# "Why D[...]
## Our Wedding, [...]"

Jill straightened her shoulders and asked it all. "Was it because of that other woman you married?"

A second of hesitation and the look in his eyes softened to something resembling guilt. "I—I..."

Reid closed his eyes to avoid seeing the raw look in Jill's. He'd noted the quick flash of darkness in them before she'd recovered and composed herself. If he hadn't known her so well...if he hadn't dreamed about those expressive eyes almost every night for the last three years, he might have missed it. Was he the cause of the pain so clearly written on her face? Even now, after all these years?

"Jill, I wanted to say I'm sorry about our wedding day. I didn't have a choice." He could barely speak, but everything inside him screamed to tell her the truth...as he knew it. But Reid only knew one incomplete part of the story himself.

Later...later he would find answers to old questions.

Dear Reader,

This season of harvest brings a cornucopia of six new passionate, powerful and provocative love stories from Silhouette Desire for your enjoyment.

Don't miss our current MAN OF THE MONTH title, Cindy Gerard's *Taming the Outlaw,* a reunion romance featuring a cowboy dealing with the unexpected consequences of a hometown summer of passion. And of course you'll want to read Katherine Garbera's *Cinderella's Convenient Husband,* the tenth absorbing title in Silhouette Desire's DYNASTIES: THE CONNELLYS continuity series.

A Navy SEAL is on a mission to win the love of the woman he left behind, in *The SEAL's Surprise Baby* by Amy J. Fetzer, while a TV anchorwoman gets up close and personal with a high-ranking soldier in *The Royal Treatment* by Maureen Child. This is the latest title in the exciting Silhouette crossline series CROWN AND GLORY.

Opposites attract when a sexy hunk and a matchmaker share digs in *Hearts Are Wild* by Laura Wright. And in *Secrets, Lies and...Passion* by Linda Conrad, a single mom is drawn into a web of desire and danger by the lover who jilted her at the altar years before...or did he?

Experience all six of these sensuous romances from Silhouette Desire this month, and guarantee that your Halloween will be all treat, no trick.

Enjoy!

*Joan Marlow Golan*

Joan Marlow Golan
Senior Editor, Silhouette Desire

Please address questions and book requests to:
Silhouette Reader Service
U.S.: 3010 Walden Ave., P.O. Box 1325, Buffalo, NY 14269
Canadian: P.O. Box 609, Fort Erie, Ont. L2A 5X3

# Secrets, Lies...
# and Passion
## LINDA CONRAD

Published by Silhouette Books
**America's Publisher of Contemporary Romance**

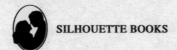 SILHOUETTE BOOKS

ISBN 0-373-76470-7

SECRETS, LIES...AND PASSION

Visit Silhouette at www.eHarlequin.com

**Printed in U.S.A.**

**Books by Linda Conrad**

Silhouette Desire

*The Cowboy's Baby Surprise* #1446
*Desperado Dad* #1458
*Secrets, Lies...and Passion* #1470

## *LINDA CONRAD*

was born in Brazil to a commercial pilot dad and a mother whose first gift was a passion for stories. She was raised in South Florida and has been a dreamer and a storyteller for as long as she can remember. Linda claims her earliest memories are of sitting in her mother's lap listening to a beloved storybook or searching through the picture books in the library to find that special one.

When Linda met and married her own dream-come-true hero, he fostered another of her other inherited vices—being a vagabond. They moved to seven different states in seven years, finally becoming enchanted with and settling down in the Rio Grande Valley of Texas.

Reality anchored Linda to their Texas home long enough to raise a daughter and become a stockbroker and certified financial planner. Her whole world suddenly changed when her widowed mother suffered a disabling stroke and Linda spent a year as her caretaker. Before her mother's second and fatal stroke, she begged Linda to go back to her dreams—to finally tell the stories buried within her heart.

Linda's hobbies are reading, growing roses and experiencing new things. However, her real passion is "passion"—reading about it, writing about it and living it. She believes that true passion and intensity for life and love are seductive—they consume the soul and make life's trials and tribulations worth all the effort.

"I am extremely grateful that today I can live my dreams by being able to share the passionate stories and lovable characters that have lived deep within me for so long," Linda declares.

To my very own real-life hero: the man who first taught me how to run aground, and then explained about getting out and pushing off once more. I love you.

# Prologue

A soft, summer breeze whispered through the star-studded Texas night, soothing Reid Sorrels's senses and cooling his heated skin. Coming to such a blissful close, this was destined to be the magical eve for a perfect wedding.

Reid rolled to his side, running a finger down the naked hip of the woman he loved and would marry in the morning. He gazed into her crystal-blue eyes, finding such promise—such deep desire. At twenty years old, Jillette Bennett was everything he'd ever wanted. Everything the twenty-four-year-old Reid figured he would ever need.

She was the first thing he thought of when he awoke and the last thing on his mind before he slept. She'd become a part of him—the best part. When he looked at her, he saw his history and his future—their children and their children's children. A never-ending union of love and trust.

He glanced at the lighted alarm clock on her nightstand and pulled her close to him once more. "It's midnight...our wedding day, Jill. You sure you don't believe it's bad luck for the groom to see the bride before the ceremony?"

"No, silly. That old wives' tale has something to do with the dress, anyway. It certainly doesn't have anything to do with what we just did." She giggled and pressed a kiss to Reid's sweat-soaked neck.

Even though they'd made love only minutes before, his sex stirred once more. He simply couldn't get enough of this raven-haired pixie who'd captured his soul. Thank God graduation was over and they had three weeks to honeymoon before he began studying for the bar exam.

Then again, he hoped he could live through three weeks of nonstop lovemaking with Jill without his body giving out on him. They were so hot together. Hot enough to sizzle fajitas on a snowy, January day.

He reached his palm to cover her breast, massaging the quivering nipple, then smiled when it pebbled against his hand. She moaned into his shoulder and pressed herself closer to him.

"You amaze me," he said with a husky catch in his throat. "You're so responsive, so uninhibited. I can't stop wanting to touch you."

"Don't stop, my darling. You were my first lover and..." She leaned over and lightly kissed his chest. "You'll be my best and last. Everything I will ever know about love comes from being with you. I want this happiness to go on and on forever."

Her body shuddered when he lowered his mouth to her breast, wet the tip with his tongue, then blew softly on the sensitive skin. "All things happen in their own time, luv," he whispered against her breast. "I should go now. You need your sleep. We have a long day ahead of us."

"No. Not just yet. Stay a few minutes more. Please?"

She lowered her hand to his rigid sex and flicked her nail across the throbbing, slick tip. Instantly, he was lost.

He swung himself over her and entered her with one, swift penetration. She moaned and threw back her head, crying his name as her internal grip tightened around him.

The fever swamped them both. She climaxed deliciously against him again and again until, with huge ragged breaths, he shattered inside her.

A half hour later, Reid left his sated, sleeping bride-to-be and tiptoed down the wide staircase toward his future father-in-law's front door. He was surprised to see Jill's cousin, Travis, standing in the shadows at the bottom of the stairs. The rehearsal party had been over for hours, but it seemed as if Travis had been waiting there to speak to him for a while. Reid wondered what could be so important.

"Travis? What's up?"

Even though they competed at everything, Travis Bennett had been his best friend for forever. Eventually, the two of them would become partners in the firm of Bennett and Bennett. Of course, by then it would hopefully be called Bennett, Bennett and Sorrels.

"Hey, buddy. Great party, wasn't it?" Travis handed him a highball glass filled with Scotch. "Can you take a minute and see my uncle? He's got something he wants to talk to you about." Travis seemed jumpy and on edge.

Reid took a big slug of the smooth fire. "What's wrong, pal? Is your father in with him?"

Travis shook his head. "Nope. Dad left a little while ago. Your soon to be father-in-law, my illustrious Uncle

Andrew, is still working in his den. He's waiting for you. Go on in. I'm just on my way out.'' Trav nodded tightly, slipped past the front door and moved out into the night.

Brothers, Jill's and Travis's fathers were also partners in the medium-size law firm. Andrew Bennett, Jill's dad, had come to the little town of Rolling Point, twenty miles outside Austin, more than thirty years ago to set up a practice. A few years later Andrew's brother, Joseph, passed the Texas bar and joined the firm. With the encroachment of the suburbs, they soon had more business than they could handle. Within a few years, the two of them built the practice up to a more than decent level.

Reid had already come to think of Andrew as a substitute father. His own distant and unemotional father was a major rancher and oilman in the area, but the two had never seen things in the same way. Even now, they couldn't manage a truce long enough to celebrate the wedding. Reid's father would not be attending tomorrow. Or was that today by now?

No matter. The idea of Andrew wanting to talk to him made Reid smile. Jill's dad was all the things Reid wanted to be—ambitious, a superlative lawyer, and a kind and loving father and husband.

Reid found the door to Andrew's den ajar. He started to push it open and walk on in, but hesitated when he heard voices. Andrew obviously had company, and Reid wasn't going to disturb them. Whatever Andrew wanted with him could wait until tomorrow.

No, on second thought, tomorrow's schedule would be so tight there'd be no time for quiet discussions. Reid stood his ground, hoping whoever was in with Andrew would soon leave.

The two voices became increasingly louder. Andrew's booming bass tone could be easily distinguished, but the other man's voice was unrecognizable. His curiosity piqued, Reid leaned into the door trying to hear more of the words.

"Our deal is private. Just between us." The strange man's voice sounded belligerent. "It's imperative that no one else knows about it...or about me."

"But my brother...and, Sorrels, my daughter's fiancé. They could be useful to us."

With the mention of Reid's name, he inched his ear closer to the opening in the door. An ominous shiver suddenly made the night cold and deadly, but he tried to shake off the feeling.

"Look," the husky, unknown voice continued. "My employers insist this deal stays secret. They wouldn't take kindly to any sudden change of plans."

The whisper of a chair scraping across carpet let Reid know the end to the conversation must be near.

The angry voice lowered to a dangerous growl. "Don't fool with us, Bennett. If you do, you won't live to regret it."

Shock and fear for his father-in-law's safety threw Reid off-balance. Before he could catch himself, he fell through the open door and landed on his knees on the plush carpet.

Reid struggled to stand. In the background, he heard Andrew's cry of surprise and a sharp curse from the stranger. But he never got a chance to get up and check on Andrew's welfare. Without warning, a crack of pain zinged across his forehead and everything around him suddenly went black.

# One

*Summer—Ten Years Later*

Jill Bennett glanced up at the gigantic gold and silver chandelier in the ballroom of the Hyatt hotel in Austin and silently prayed for patience. The big-haired, big-bosomed woman speaking to her droned on in a twanging, West Texas drawl. As one of the largest political contributors in the entire northern part of the state, the woman was too important for Jill to duck entirely.

"Now, sugar," the rhinestone-studded woman continued, while loading a cracker with a huge dollop of caviar. "You must let me throw you and Billy a Texas-size—" she crammed the cracker into her mouth but didn't stop talking "—wedding shower."

Jill couldn't understand much of what she was saying with her mouth stuffed the way it was.

Spewing cracker crumbs with every word, the woman went on. "I know all the best movers and shakers in the state. You do realize it's the wives who make most of the contribution decisions, don't you?"

Jill nodded but didn't manage to get in one word before the older woman was swept to the other side of the buffet table by a crowd of Stetson-hatted men. Jill took the opportunity to move away from the table and the boisterous crowd. She scooted around the twelve-foot ice sculpture of a long-horned bull and found a relatively quiet corner.

Looking down at the sparkling, two-karat diamond on her finger, she swallowed back the urge to scream. How dare Bill Baldwin place an engagement ring on her finger in front of a room full of contributors without the slightest hint to her in advance?

*What had possessed him?*

The man was the ultimate politician. She glanced over at him, across the crowded room, as he shook hands with the governor, accepting congratulations all around for his newly announced engagement—to her. With his blond hair slicked back from his forehead in the latest style, his tastefully understated designer suit and his outlandishly expensive tie, Bill was the very picture of the fair-haired boy in state government. As the Texas attorney general and darling of the media, he'd be next in line for the governor's mansion.

But why would the man, who had privately professed his love for her, pick an impersonal, crowded and noisy political fund-raiser to announce their engagement when she hadn't even said yes yet? Shaking her head, she tried to dismiss the thought that it had been just a political stunt. Could Bill really stoop so low?

"Congratulations, Jill." Her cousin Travis, now a state

senator and her partner in Bennett and Bennett, arrived at her side, leaned down and kissed her cheek. "I hope you'll be very happy."

"Uh..."

She really didn't know what to say. Oh, she'd figured Bill would pop the question sooner or later, but her heart refused to deliver an answer. Bill had been a good friend, and her son, Andy, seemed to like him well enough. Still...when Jill kissed him, she felt—comfortable. Not disgusted or repulsed certainly, but neither did she feel anything like love or passion. It was more like—kissing a brother—or maybe like kissing Travis.

Her cousin Travis, as youthful-looking as ever, despite his many obligations, handed her a glass of champagne. Close up, she saw, along with the freckles across the bridge of his nose, a few wrinkles at the corners of his eyes. He looked exhausted. Perhaps the stress of running the family's law partnership and also being a state legislator was beginning to take its toll on him.

Smiling at how often in their lives she'd wished he'd been her brother, Jill sighed against his pinstripe-suited shoulder for a quick moment. "I still haven't given him an answer, Trav. I'm just not sure what I..." With her thoughts a jumble, she hesitated. Stepping back, she took a sip from her glass, and gazed into her cousin's electric blue eyes. She knew they matched her own, and the thought gave her some comfort. Since her father's death and her uncle's massive stroke, Travis had been the one rock in her life.

"I've talked to you about this until I'm purple in the face." Travis raised his eyebrow and started ticking off reasons. "You need a husband. Andy needs a father. You helped get Bill elected. He owes you. What more do you need?"

"Those are hardly reasons enough to get married." Jill downed her glass and placed it on the tray of a passing waiter. "After all, I helped get you elected, too. If you weren't already married, would you expect me to marry you too, cuz?"

He rolled his eyes to the ceiling in frustration. "Very funny. You know I love you, Jill. I'm just trying to look out for your welfare." He drained his glass and set it aside. "Look. Why don't you take a few days and think it over?"

Respect for her cousin and confusion over what would be the right thing to do for everyone concerned left her momentarily silent. She nodded her head.

"All right, Trav. I won't make a decision about marrying him...not until I think about it, anyhow."

"That's my girl." Travis eased his arm around her shoulder and gave her a bear hug. "Uh, I have something else to tell you."

Jill's feet were suddenly throbbing and her head hurt. Judging by the troubled look on her cousin's face, whatever he had to say was going to mean more problems.

She stepped away to face him squarely. "This isn't about the business, is it? 'Cause if it is, can't it wait until tomorrow?"

"No. This isn't about business, cuz." Travis looked down at his spit-shined shoes. That really worried her. It wasn't like her cousin to be tentative in any way. What was going on?

Finally, Travis raised his gaze to look at her. "I've brought someone along with me tonight. I didn't think you'd mind, or maybe that you'd be too busy to even notice. But I also didn't know about Bill's surprise announcement." He turned to glance around the room. "The two things don't go together at all. I'm sorry, Jill."

"Travis, what on earth are you talkin..."

"Hello, Jill."

If Reid hadn't stepped into her view right then, she still would've known who he was just by his voice. She'd heard that deep, resonant bass tone in her dreams and nightmares nearly every night for the last ten years.

And then...there he was.

Before her stood a stranger with her former lover's eyes. She tried to take in every inch of the man without being too obvious.

He was about the same height as the man she remembered, but nothing else physically seemed familiar. His hair, always a warm brown and silkily soft, had tinges of silver sprinkled throughout, making him look much older than the thirty-four she knew he must be. He no longer had the slender, rail-thin frame of late adolescence. Instead, his shoulders were broad and muscular under the tobacco-colored cotton sweater he wore atop his casual khakis.

This was a real adult male standing here, glaring at her. She took one more second to study his face. The beautiful, patrician nose and jaw she could remember tenderly kissing had been replaced by rugged features and fractured lines. The boy that had captured her heart was gone. In his place, stood a man of considerable power and character.

She tried to steady her rapid heartbeat. "Reid." Her voice came out high-pitched and squeaky as she fought for calm.

"Yeah. Like the proverbial bad penny, I've turned up again just at the wrong time."

He took her hand in both of his, driving electrical charges through her arm and straight into her soul. "You look great, Jill. Time has been very kind to you."

Reid pinned her with a steady scrutiny, making her squirm internally. "Well, I suppose turning up at a bad time is better than disappearing at the absolute worst possible moment," she mumbled with a fake smile.

She involuntarily jerked on her hand, trying to free herself from his grip, but all the while she continued to meet his gaze. It cost her more than he'd ever know to stand there touching him with outward calm.

Despite her attempts to break free, he didn't let her go or acknowledge her dig. "Congratulations on your engagement. I apologize for putting a damper on your big night, but all Travis told me was we were going to a political fund-raiser for members of the state legislature and some of our old classmates. He didn't bother to tell me you'd be here, let alone what kind of shindig this was really going to be." He gave the other man a pointed look.

Jill was so engrossed in his eyes that she barely heard what he said. Those eyes were still as black and intense as she remembered—only even more so.

He finally released her and she dragged her hand away, waving it with a casual flair she didn't feel. "It's not Travis's fault. None of us knew what was going to happen…except Bill, of course. And he decided to keep it a secret."

"Uh. Excuse me, you two, but there are some constituents I have to speak to," Travis broke into the strained lull in the conversation. "I'll find you when I'm ready to leave, Reid. And I'll talk to you in the morning, cuz." Travis spun and went into his politician's mode, greeting people with a handshake and a colossal smile.

Reid was furious with his boyhood friend. *Damn that Travis anyway.* How could he not mention that Jill would be here? All Travis had talked about before the party were the good "contacts" Reid could make with his old law-school buddies at this fund-raiser.

As FBI special agent in charge of Operation Rock-A-Bye, Reid had reluctantly returned to his hometown on the outskirts of Austin, ostensibly to attend his ten-year, law-school reunion and to spend time with his mother and his old buddies. In reality, this trip was a cover.

He'd fervently wished for some other way to track down the head of the international baby-selling ring that they'd traced to the state legislature in Austin. But this reunion was too perfect.

For years he'd been after the bastard who'd ruined countless lives on both sides of the border. A few months ago, one of his undercover special agents had apprehended one of the middlemen in the ring. Under interrogation, the man had admitted he didn't know the main boss of the illegal operation but all his contacts had been through Austin, and those men were definitely on the outskirts of politics.

Reid hadn't been back to Rolling Point once in ten years. Not even when his father died. For the last few years, he'd managed to avoid the very thought of home and his lost opportunities and disappointments.

He certainly didn't want to be here now, but he was the best man for this job. A full three-quarters of his law school class was serving in some government capacity. All of them would remember his name. He could have access to things no other agent involved in Operation Rock-A-Bye would.

Using Travis to introduce him into the inner circles of the state legislature had, at first, seemed like the fastest way to ferret out the man he hunted. Now he wished for any other way. Travis had tricked him into coming face-to-face with the main reason he'd never returned before this—the main reason he ached when he thought of home.

"You look great, Jill." It killed Reid to get the words out, but they were the simple truth.

He mentally tried to steel himself against Jill's presence. His temples pounded with the hurt of seeing her again. The sweat beaded up and began to trickle down his chest under his shirt. He fought for some of his famous control. After all these years, the conflict he felt between wanting to hurt her and wanting to ravage her on the nearest table nearly finished him off.

*She* was supposed to be the impulsive and conflicted one. After that fateful night ten years ago, she'd been the one who had run off to Paris and got married before he could come back and explain what had happened.

To this day, Reid wasn't exactly positive himself about what happened on the eve of their wedding. Oh, he'd thought about it until his brain was weary. But some of the memories were gone forever. After he'd been hit in the head, he apparently was beaten bloody and left for dead two hundred miles away from home. Memories from the time he was unconscious refused to be captured.

It was a couple of months later before he was capable of speaking or piecing any of his shattered memories together. By then it was too late. The trail was cold. The only person that might have told him what happened, Jill's father, was already dead. And Jill had left the country.

From that disappointment, he'd learned the hard way how to detach and control. So why was he having so much trouble being close to her now? He should still hate her for not caring enough about him to go looking for him when he'd disappeared. But he didn't. Not by a long shot.

"Thanks," she said softly. "You look pretty good yourself. It's been a long time."

Within the space of a heartbeat, all the memories of her came flooding back. She looked much the same as she had at fifteen when he'd first met her and fell in love.

Still petite with those wide, flashing blue eyes, the only differences he could find in her were tiny little lines in the corners of her eyes and a figure that was more rounded than little-girlish. But those differences made her even more appealing than she'd been at twenty. Even in a navy business suit, she had a woman's sensuality about her that clawed at his gut and left him breathless and turned on.

He fisted his hands and tried a half-hearted grin. "My mother told me you'd been divorced a while back. I guess she didn't realize you were involved with someone again."

She looked confused at his words. "Involved?" Quickly, she appeared to recover as she glanced down at the oversized diamond ring on her finger. "Oh, you mean..."

"Involved. You know...like engaged?"

She looked up at him with that same vulnerable look she'd had at nineteen when he'd just asked her to marry him.

At that instant, he'd known she was the only woman for him. Eleven years and a lifetime of pain later, she was still the only woman for him. But it could never happen. Worlds apart, their lives now traveled far different paths. It would be impossible to breach the chasm.

But knowing that fact and being able to control his wayward body were drastically opposing ideas. He took a deep breath and was instantly sorry. The scent of her assailed his nostrils, filling him with the sweet smell of herbs that had always been her signature fragrance.

And nearly knocking him down with memories.

The memory of her standing naked at a closet door and turning to smile, blinded him with emotion. The ghostly remembrance of her hair's springy curls wrapped tightly around his fingers while they'd kissed, made his lips tingle with need and his fingers itch with desire.

He closed his eyes. He wasn't sure if he wanted to capture those memories and keep them, or if he'd rather shut himself off against them.

"Engaged. Uh. Yeah," she stammered. "Well, it took me by surprise as well."

The mention of an engagement had rocketed Jill back in time. To the sweetness of being in love and preparing to marry the man of her dreams. To the pain of being rejected and left before she could make it to the altar. To the desperation of later trying to find Reid when she'd learned she was pregnant.

It all came back with a horrifying rip at her heart. The spoiled child she'd always been grew up in a hurry that year. Even her dear, doting father had changed into a tyrant overnight. A few weeks after Reid disappeared on the morning of their wedding, she'd confessed her pregnancy to her father. She'd begged him to help find Reid. Instead, he ranted and claimed the man was no good anyway, then sent her out of town to face her mistakes alone.

She'd always had a feeling her father had known more about what happened to Reid than he'd let on, but before she could return and press him for answers, her father was killed in a car accident. Whatever he'd known died with him.

Later, after she'd returned home with her son and with a story her mother made up for appearances' sake, Jill learned that Reid had married someone else. She imagined that woman must have been why he'd left in the first place and her pride suffered greatly.

But life went on. There was someone else now who needed her and loved her. Her beautiful son, the light of her life and the reason the pain of losing Reid had faded to a dull ache.

At the moment, however, she was stunned to find that just looking at Reid brought the pain back so clearly. It was sharp enough after ten years to nearly double her over. Dear heavens. She had to get a grip on herself. But she also had to ask the big question—and right this minute.

"Why did you leave me before our wedding, Reid?" She straightened her shoulders and asked it all. "Was it because of that other woman Mother later told me you'd married?"

He suddenly looked stricken, like he'd swallowed something the wrong way. "God, no," he choked.

A second's hesitation and the look in his eyes softened to something resembling quilt. "I...I..."

Reid closed his eyes to avoid seeing the raw look in Jill's. He'd noted the quick flash of darkness in them before she'd recovered and composed herself. If he hadn't known her so well...if he hadn't dreamed about those expressive eyes almost every night for the last ten years, he might have missed it.

His first reaction was that the flash had been pain—or maybe anguish. But why? After all this time, why would thinking back to that time cause her anything more than a bit of regret? Hell, they'd both just been kids, and she obviously hadn't cared as much as he'd thought she had.

He reached out a hand to steady her shoulder and give himself a little balance as well. What he really wanted was to give her strength through his touch and make her life easier, but he didn't know why he felt that way.

Was he the cause of some of the pain so clearly written on her face? Even now, after all these years?

"Jill, I wanted to say I'm sorry about our wedding day. I didn't have a choice..." He could barely speak.

Everything inside him screamed to tell her the truth as he knew it. "I had to leave. It wasn't something I planned. But I can't...I don't want to talk about it."

Not telling her about being knocked unconscious and left for dead hundreds of miles away would be one of the toughest things he'd ever done. But Reid only knew one incomplete part of the story himself, and that part involved her father. It might be more than she could stand to hear now that he was dead. Anyway, Reid was sure it couldn't possibly matter *much* to her. Otherwise, why hadn't she come looking for him?

"Why? Why can't you talk about it?" she demanded. "Don't I deserve an explanation?"

"Jill, please. It over. Nothing we say can change the outcome. Let's just go on." He heard his own voice getting lower and rougher. "Was that day so terrible for you?" he asked in a hoarse whisper.

"No, not at all. My father took care of everything for me. He was wonderful. That morning, before I left for the church, he told me you'd changed your mind. He said you'd written me a note but that he'd ripped it up in anger. I understood exactly how he felt."

A look of pure steel entered her eyes as Reid saw the memories overtake her. "Poor Dad. He spent all day notifying guests and cancelling the arrangements. His whole staff pitched in to make sure presents were returned and apologies made. After I took off my wedding dress and explained things to my bridesmaids, I had very little to do."

*Right, good old Dad to the rescue.* Why had her father, the man Reid had idolized, betrayed him? Automatically, the old questions welled up inside him. He pushed them aside and reminded himself that he was a different man now, and that his current FBI sting operation had to take precedence over his past. Later. Later he would find answers to old questions.

"That's what your father told you? That I'd just changed my mind about marrying you? And you believed him?"

She jerked her shoulder out of his grasp. "Of course, why would my father lie to me? That's what your letter said. Although, I always thought it was kind of obvious by the fact that you weren't there for the wedding."

"But didn't you think I owed you an explanation in person? You didn't bother trying to find me. Why not?"

Reid noticed Jill's focus wavering and she glanced around the room for the first time since they'd been standing together in this corner. Why would that question make her so nervous?

"I thought you said nothing could change the outcome now. Why talk about this?" she asked. "Besides, Dad said you'd left for good. I didn't know where to start looking.

"Dad and Mom suggested I go off to finish undergraduate school at the Sorbonne in Paris shortly after that day, and by the time I returned the whole thing had blown over."

Despite her pride, he could feel her anguish. She'd been so spoiled back then—Daddy's little girl. Reid truly wasn't surprised she'd given up on him so quickly. It didn't help his pride much, however. He didn't want to feel sorry for her now. He'd spent enough time feeling sorry for himself.

"I suppose we were the talk of the town for a while, but neither of us was around to be bothered by the gossip," she concluded.

He wanted to blurt out the truth. To tell her everything he could remember. To force her to believe it wasn't his fault, even though his story might sound fantastic.

But he couldn't. He was petrified that by destroying her father's image he might be destroying her as well.

"I understand your father was killed in a car crash a few weeks later. Didn't you come back for his funeral?" he asked instead.

"No. I... I was very busy with school and midterms at the time. Mother and I had a quiet memorial together when I got home. It was really much easier on me to grieve for him in private."

His gut told him that was her second lie of the night. Something more was underlying her words, but he decided to let it pass...for now.

"Is your wife with you on this trip?" she asked.

"We've been divorced for many years now, Jill."

"Oh?" She hesitated, once again glancing away for a second. "So why are you back here after all this time?"

Reid opened his eyes to the thirty-year-old woman she'd become and studied a wayward tendril of hair that had escaped her attempts at a twist at the back of her head. Instead of scholarly and professional, which was the look he figured she'd been going for, the effect was electrifying in its innocent sensuality.

Her question brought him back to reality with a thump. "I'm back for my ten-year, law-school reunion."

"Are you staying with Travis then?" Jill blinked and straightened.

Reid shook his head to answer her, but decided to watch her carefully for any flashes of emotions he didn't want to miss. "I'm out on the ranch with Mom. I've decided to take a little time off. Use this opportunity to revisit some of my old friends. Get reacquainted with Mom."

"Time off from what, Reid? Where are you working?"

For an answer, he went right into his undercover mode with no trouble. "I work for the federal government. I head up a compliance agency for the Treasury Department."

Her surprised look was clearer than the last fleeting emotion in her eyes had been. "You're a bureaucrat? What happened to the law? You were always so sure of what you wanted to do with your life. What changed?"

He shrugged a shoulder. "I guess I was just young and full of some misguided sense of justice. Reality intruded."

She was different from most civilians. He felt he had to say something more to her than he might say to anyone else. Even though the whole cover story was basically a lie, he let a little bit of the truth sneak out.

"After a few hard hits in life," he began softly. "We all make our way the best we can, Jill. Enough pain, and eventually you end up taking the easiest, least stressful route to get what you want."

She nodded once. "Yes. Enough pain will change your entire outlook. That's a fact." Looking uncomfortable, she quickly changed the subject. "I'd better find my *fiancé*."

Her words knifed through him, stopping him cold for a second. But he was a big, bad special agent in charge for the FBI. He couldn't let anything so personal throw him off track. Especially not something that he had no control over—nor any right to dispute.

Grimacing inwardly, he squared his shoulders and tried for equanimity. "Sure thing. How about introducing me to him? I'm really anxious to meet this young, rising star I've been hearing so much about."

# Two

On the way home in the car with Bill a couple hours later, Jill couldn't stop thinking about the look in Reid's eyes. *Damn him.* He'd been the one to leave her standing at the altar. What right did he have to be hurt at the mention of her new engagement?

None. Zip. Nada. He'd given up those rights when he disappeared and quickly married someone else.

And why in the world had he questioned her so intensely about her trying to find him back then? The truth was that the morning sickness had stopped her. That and her pride. But she sure as heck wasn't going to mention either of those things to him.

Jill hadn't been so sure that introducing her former fiancé to the man who fancied himself to be her current one was the smartest thing. But since Bill had walked up to them just at the moment Reid had asked to meet him, she'd been stuck. She'd plastered on her best fund-raising smile and gotten through it.

The thing was—she'd been horrified to find that she couldn't take her eyes off of Reid. Bill's reactions or lack of them hadn't mattered one bit. Her biggest concern had been Reid's feelings. She'd seen the fleeting look of pain in his eyes when she'd mentioned Bill, and it had chipped away a piece of her soul.

Jill shook her head to disengage the unwanted thoughts and realized Bill had been asking her a question. Fortunately, he hadn't taken his eyes off the road long enough to catch her inattention. Maybe she could cover.

"Excuse me, Bill. Could you repeat that? I was just thinking back to how surprised I was when you pulled out that ring tonight."

He stole a quick glance at her out of the corner of his eye. "What's wrong with you this evening, sweetheart? You're so distracted you don't even listen when I'm trying to cajole you into going away for a weekend with me."

Now he had her full attention. "We've talked about this many times, Bill. You know my feelings about sex before marriage. I'm trying to set a good example for my son. I don't want him to grow up to be irresponsible or to ruin his future by getting some stranger pregnant."

She found herself squirming in her seat. Her words had a particularly hollow sound this evening and she wondered if Bill noticed.

"Yes, but now that we're engaged I thought perhaps you could relax your rules a bit. You wouldn't even have to tell Andy we're together. You could just call it a business trip or something."

"Hmm. More like monkey business." She folded her

arms over her chest. "No. That wouldn't be the honorable thing to do."

Something about this conversation was nagging at her, but Jill just couldn't get a grasp on what it was.

"Besides, I still haven't said yes to your proposal," she insisted.

"But you accepted my ring. You let me announce our engagement in front of all those contributors. Of course you're going to marry me."

"I didn't 'let' you do anything, Bill. You were the one who decided to turn the fund-raiser into a surprise engagement party." She turned to stare out the window. "By the way, I don't appreciate you springing such a personal thing on me in such a public way."

"Oh, come on. You know a politician's life is in the public eye. You'd better get used to being in the spotlight. After we're married, nearly everything we do will have public relations overtones. The governor's wife doesn't have a life of her own."

"Yes, but we're not married, and you're not the governor...yet. This is a big step for me. I have a lot of things to consider. Not the least of which is whether I want my son to have his whole life exposed to the public's view."

"Well, think fast. Late summer will be a perfect time for our wedding and you'll need to get busy with the details. We'll time it to coincide with the announcement of my candidacy. It'll be great PR to kick off the campaign."

Jill sighed inwardly. What was wrong with her, anyway? Marrying Bill made perfect sense. He was a man destined for great things and she loved working behind the scenes of politics. He seemed genuinely fond of her and Andy, and her son certainly needed a man's influence in his life right now.

If her father had been alive, he would have been pleased at their union. Her father loved politics and having a son-in-law in the governor's mansion would have made up for some of the disappointments Jill had given him.

But this was going way too fast for her. She simply refused to be pushed into agreeing to something so monumental without giving it time to sink in.

"Please slow things down a little, Bill. Andy has to be my first consideration. In fact…" She slid the ring off her finger and slipped it into his coat pocket. "I want to talk to him about this before I even start wearing your ring. Try to have some patience with me. I'll come to the right decision for all of us in the end."

"Oh, I wouldn't even let you out of my sight if I doubted for one minute that this time next year you'll be my campaign manager and wife. So I'll wait for a while, but not very patiently, I'm afraid."

He turned his head to flash his dentist-enhanced, white teeth. "Please don't make me wait too long. Remember, we have a great future ahead of us, Jill."

If that were true, how come she felt so bleak and empty at just the thought of what lay ahead of her? Yes, this decision would take a lot of soul searching and introspection. Something she hadn't attempted since the only man she'd ever loved had walked out of her life on the day of their marriage and never returned.

Now she would be forced to take a look inside herself just when that same man had stepped back into her conscious mind—and, unbidden, was slowly seeping back into her heart.

* * *

A few days after having to face Jill at that fateful political fund-raiser, Reid shoved the old, straw work hat back off his forehead and ran a sweaty palm across his eyes. It had been so long since he'd done any ranch work that he'd forgotten how hot and dry it could be.

And it didn't help things one bit that he couldn't concentrate on settling his mother's bull into his temporary new home due to thinking about Jill Bennett and the way she'd looked the other night at the fund-raiser. If he had to be thinking about things besides manhandling a two-ton Brangus, he should've been trying to sort out some of the potential suspects for Operation Rock-A-Bye that he'd run into over the last few days—not lollygagging about a woman lost to him long ago.

"That should just about do 'er, Mr. Sorrels." The young ranch hand closed the bull pen gate and grinned at Reid. "Ol' Pete will begin his 'donations' work tomorrow. Don't you worry about him none. We'll have him back to you by end of next week—just as good as he is today. The vet'll see to it."

"That's just fine, Bobby Ray. I'm sure Pete will enjoy his stay." Reid slanted the kid his own version of a grin. "Now, can you fetch Sonny for me to sign the papers? The insurance company insists the Double B has to take formal delivery of Pete or their policy won't cover the temporary move."

"Sorry, Mr. Sorrels." Bobby Ray squinted up at Reid and covered his eyes, blocking the shaft of sun that hit him square in the face. "Sonny had to go over to San Angelo today for the quarter horse auction. He won't be back till late. He said for you to go on up to the house and have Miz Bennett sign whatever you need."

*Damn.* Now what?

The only reason Reid had agreed to run this errand

was because he was sure he wouldn't need to deal with Jill's mother. His own mother had insisted that he could just deliver the bull to the Double B, have the foreman sign the insurance forms and leave. He wasn't supposed to have to face the woman who probably hated him more than dirt for leaving her daughter standing at the altar.

*Well, shoot.*

Reid's mother had made a kind of peace with the Bennetts over the years. Once both the mothers had become widows, they'd even begun to do business together. Between them, they now ran two of the most profitable ranches in ten counties. Reid was proud of his mother, but right now, he could just strangle her.

Finally, he shrugged with resignation, grabbed the papers from the truck and headed toward the main house. When the front door opened to admit him, it was not Mrs. Bennett who'd answered the bell.

Before him stood a good-looking young boy. The nearly five-foot-high, dark-eyed and rather sullen child stared silently up at him. Reid couldn't have been more surprised if someone took a shot at him.

"Well hey, partner. And…just who might you be?" Reid sputtered.

"Whatta you want?" the kid bounced back at him.

Reid removed his hat and studied the boy. "Yeah, okay. I guess that's a fair question. My name is Reid Sorrels and I need to see Mrs. Bennett about some papers for the bull I just delivered."

"Sorrels? You related to Miz Sorrels over to the Sorrels' ranch?"

"I'm her son. May I come in?"

The boy stood his ground for a second then backed up a step to admit Reid to the house. Reid slowly stepped over the threshold, using the time to speculate about just who this child might be. He was a good-looking, rail-thin preteen, with black, curly hair and eyes that made Reid think of shadows in the dead of night.

The young boy was dressed in jeans and a work shirt, with his oversized feet stuffed into cowboy boots that looked well scuffed and worn. With those feet, this kid was bound to grow into a pro basketball player.

Just who was he anyway? He didn't look like he belonged to the Bennetts, who were all blue-eyed and petite. Even Jill's father had been of relatively short stature for a man. Maybe this kid belonged to the foreman, or perhaps to some of the household help?

"You wait in there," the child said, pointing toward the huge great room that took up the entire front half of the house. "I'll go get Nana."

With that remark, the boy took off toward the far reaches of the ranch house. Did he say 'Nana'? Good Lord. Could this be Jill's boy? But that was impossible. This child looked to be ten or eleven, and it was only ten years ago next week that Reid and Jill's wedding would have taken place. She certainly hadn't had a kid back then.

In fact, Reid remembered his mother telling him that Jill married a Frenchman, had his son and was divorced a few years after she'd left town. That should make this kid more like seven or eight. Maybe the boy was already a giant for his age?

But then, what Reid knew about kids could fit into the point end of a hollow-nosed bullet.

He was still working on the incongruent appearance of the child when he heard a noise behind him.

"What do you want here, Reid?" The sound of Jill's voice startled him out of his reverie.

He turned to face her. "Oh, hi. I…I brought over Ol'

Pete as a favor for Mom. The foreman's out of town, so I need to get your mother's signature on these insurance papers.'' He held them out as if to prove he wasn't telling a lie.

Staring down at his outstretched hand, she focused on the papers like they were contaminated. Jill looked absolutely fantastic today. With no makeup and in her stocking feet, the too-tight jeans and scarlet cropped-top she wore made her look ten years younger. The coal-black hair she'd tried desperately to tame the other night flew free in a cloud of curls around her face and down her back.

She stood frozen to the spot. What had he said that was so hard to understand?

Reid cleared his throat. ''Uh. Didn't expect to see you here, Jill. Travis told me you had a house in Rolling Point near your office.''

He pulled the papers back to his side and waited for her gaze to find his. When she finally glanced up at him, he was dumbfounded to find a look of pure panic in her eyes.

She finally seemed to find her voice, but didn't answer his questions. ''Give me the papers. I'll take them to Mother. You wait here.''

''But…''

''Mom! Mo…ooom!'' The sound of boots clacking on wooden floorboards filled the entry way. Within a second, the young boy who'd greeted him at the door came barreling around a corner. ''Oh. There you are. Nana says to bring the guy back to her office.''

''Andy!'' Jill grabbed up her son and pulled him to her. Reid watched as a dozen different expressions ran across her face.

He tried to sort through what he saw in her eyes, but

the overwhelming impression she gave was that she was scared to death. Reid narrowed his eyes to watch her more closely. What was going on in that beautiful and super-smart head of hers anyway?

He looked down on her as she gently pushed back a lock of shiny hair from the boy's forehead and Reid noted her tremendous struggle for calm.

"Andy," she whispered. "Say hello to Reid Sorrels. He's an old friend and neighbor."

The boy turned to Reid while his mother stood stiffly behind him with one hand on his shoulder.

"Reid, this is my son Andy Bennett. We're staying out here with Mom for his summer vacation."

So this boy was really her son. Named Andy after his dead grandfather and going by the name of Bennett? Reid's split second of hesitation caused Jill to draw in a breath. What was the problem with her?

Reid promptly stuck out his hand. "Pleased to meet you, son. How're ya doing?"

The child's wary eyes relaxed slightly as he quickly moved to shake hands. "How do you do, sir?" The kid had an impressive grip.

Reid's gaze moved from the boy to his mother, but her face had become a mask. Suddenly, the woman he'd always thought of as an open book became a mystery.

"Are you a cowboy?" Andy's question jerked Reid's attention back to the youngster.

"I want to be a cowboy when I grow up. I already know how to ride, and I practice my roping every day. You ever been to a rodeo? I'm going to be a big star there someday."

Reid couldn't help but grin at the boy. "Yes, I've been to the rodeo. In fact, I rode the broncs there sometimes, but it's been many years ago."

"Mr. Sorrels is being modest," Jill said with a smile aimed at the back of her son's head. "He won several titles on the circuit as a teenager, Andy. He was quite the rodeo star."

"Really? Cool!" The kid's whole face lit up. "But I wanna be a calf-roper when I grow up."

"Maybe I could give you a few pointers some day," Reid said to the earnest youngster. "I used to have a fairly steady hand with the calves."

"Would you? Wow. That would be so cool, wouldn't it, Mom?"

Jill shook her head at Reid with a grimace, but she softened the look as the boy turned to her with wide, pleading eyes. "I don't think Mr. Sorrels really has the time to work with you," she murmured. "Besides you're too young to practice on the real thing. We've talked about this before."

"But, he said…" Andy whined.

"Andy, let me talk to your mother about this a bit, son. Maybe we can work out a compromise." Reid was surprised how his own voice gentled. "For right now, though, why don't you show me where your Nana's office is? I need to get on back to my mother's ranch with these papers."

"Yes, sir." The boy straightened and looked so deadly serious Reid almost pulled him to his chest for a hug. "I hope you and Mom can work out a com-proo-mise. I'll be real good. I promise." Andy turned and took off toward the rear of the ranch house.

Jill laid her hand on Reid's arm to stop him as he began following Andy's path. "It was very kind of you to offer to help him," she whispered. "But I know how busy you must be. Don't think that you have to live up to some offer you made in haste. He'll be okay."

She'd left her hand on his forearm. Instead of answering her right away, Reid looked down at the spot where she touched him. Urgent sensations of smoldering heat and flaming desire spread out along his skin and raced directly to his gut.

When he could finally raise his gaze, her eyes widened in surprise. Something distinctly sexual and enormously intense passed between them. Jill jerked her hand back and dragged it through her hair in a nervous and self-conscious move. Suddenly, Reid's brain felt scrambled and for the life of him he couldn't remember what she'd just said.

"Don't worry. I'll explain things to Andy," she mumbled, pulling her hand back to her side. "For now, do you want me to get Mother to sign those papers for you?"

Andy? Oh, yeah…the boy. There was still something drastically wrong here. Maybe it had to do with the kid's father.

"Jill, I want to help him with his roping. It would make me happy. He seems like a good kid. A little too serious and sincere maybe, but he reminds me of me at that age."

Another series of varying emotions ran across her face, and Reid wanted badly to get to the bottom of the trouble—whatever it was. "How often does his father get to see him?" he asked. "Can he teach the boy anything about ranching or roping?"

"His father doesn't… His father doesn't ever see him. He's cut him out of his life for good."

"I'm sorry. Boys need a father…to learn how to become men." Reid watched as Jill's demeanor became tense and nervous once again. "How about your fiancé? Can he teach him the things he needs to know?"

"No. Bill is a very busy man. He and Andy get along okay, but he can't spend much time with him."

"Too bad. Boys need..."

She waved off his words. "He has plenty of men around the ranch to emulate, and Travis tries to spend time with him. The reality is he has me to be both his mother and his father. He'll do just fine." Her hands fluttered in front of her with distressingly jerky movements.

"Do you have any boys of your own?" she asked.

He sadly shook his head. "The marriage was a mistake from the beginning. Fortunately, we didn't compound the error by having children."

"I'm sorry. I know how much you wanted..."

"Um, yeah," he said hastily. "But getting back to Andy, unless you can give me a real good reason why you don't want him to learn anything about rodeoing, I'd like to spend a little time with him. Show him a few tricks. I have the time and I can't think of a better way to kill a little of it."

The pain of Jill's betrayal had faded over the years, at least enough to make him care if she was in trouble. A deep curiosity, born from years of being an undercover agent, fueled his concern.

There was more than one mystery for him to solve around his old stomping grounds. He was determined to give both the mother and the child enough time to find out what was behind Jill's strange behavior. He would know the truth. It was only a matter of time.

After the papers were duly signed and Reid had left the ranch, Jill stood facing her mother's inquisition.

"Why didn't you tell me Reid was back in town?" Caroline Bennett demanded.

Jill sighed and plopped down on the leather sofa in her mother's office. "I didn't think it was important. He's just here for his law-school reunion. He'll be gone soon."

"Not important? The man caused this family undefinable pain and disgrace. Now he shows up on our doorstep and you don't think that's important?"

"Mother, please." Jill knew dramatics were her mother's stock in trade, but she'd hoped her newfound confidence at becoming a good rancher would have tempered them somewhat. No such luck.

At nearly sixty, Caroline was still what could be called a "raving" beauty. She always was a bit disappointed that Jill had been born short with unruly hair and startling blue eyes instead of being sleek, sophisticated and gorgeous like herself.

Jill's attitude only made the disappointment worse. Today, for instance, Jill was in old jeans and battered tank top, while Caroline wore a leather skirt and vest, tailored denim blouse and stylish high-heeled boots.

"Please, what? Is it too much for me to be concerned about my only daughter and my only grandson's welfare?"

"No, Mom. Concern is good. Overreacting is bad. Reid's only going to be here for a while. Besides, you and his mother have made peace enough to do business together, why shouldn't Reid and I make peace as well?"

"You know perfectly well why. He's the one person on earth who could cause you more pain. You can make 'peace' with him all you want, but if he ever finds out the truth... Well, I'm afraid even your hard-earned, University of Texas law degree wouldn't keep him from making your life miserable...and just when you're about to snag the most eligible bachelor in the whole state of Texas."

Jill took a deep breath. It wasn't as if she herself hadn't thought of these things, but to hear her mother speak them aloud, made the whole deal with Bill sound sordid.

"I'm not about to *snag* anyone. Bill asked me to marry him. I haven't decided whether I want to be his wife yet."

At her mother's stricken look, she hurried to get out the rest of the bad news.

"Reid wants to spend some time with Andy."

Caroline looked horrified so Jill quickly continued. "Oh no, he doesn't have any idea about the truth." At least, she prayed he didn't. "Andy asked him to help with his roping and Reid told him he would. That's all there is to it."

"You're not going to permit it, are you?" Her mother found her voice again.

"I really have no choice. If I made a big fuss, Reid would want to know why."

Jill knew disaster with Reid was potentially only a few misspoken words away. She would never lie to Reid about his son, though she wasn't quite ready to admit the whole truth either. But she had an even bigger concern.

"I really don't want Andy to start asking the wrong questions. I don't want to tell my son any more lies."

"He's a baby, Jill. He's too young to understand. You told him the same story we told everyone else. Why change things now?"

"Oh, Mother." Jill stood, heading for the door and fresh air. "Andy is not a baby anymore. I don't want him to figure it out before I get a chance to explain things."

"Then for heaven's sake keep them separated."

"They have a right to get to know each other. It'll be fine. What could happen?"

# Three

————

"**W**hy are you so interested in Jill? I thought you made it clear ten years ago that you couldn't care less about her." Travis rested his elbows on the solid wood of the old neighborhood bar. He raised a longneck beer to his lips and took a swig while studying Reid over the bottom of the amber-colored bottle.

Reid took a careful and calculated sip from his own bottle. Although he and Travis had been best buddies once, they hadn't contacted one another in ten years. At first, in the hospital, it had been impossible for Reid to contact anyone. Then, as time went on, he didn't want any reminders of that earlier period in his life—those kind of thoughts only brought depression and frustration. So Reid deliberately stayed away, letting people think whatever they wanted about him and his reasons for leaving.

But now he needed Travis. Oh, he wouldn't be letting

Trav in on the truth of who he was or his real reason for coming back. But Reid could make up something to satisfy his old buddy. Travis was his ticket to the legislature.

So far, Reid met or had been reintroduced to a couple dozen of the lawmakers. He felt comfortable enough with them to share a few beers and surreptitiously ask most of the questions he wanted. But that wasn't all he needed. His job demanded he ask intricate questions about political procedures and the internal processes that go into a legislator's life.

Operation Rock-A-Bye's main suspect had to be an attorney as well as a politician. A man that would also have access to politicians from across the border. He would have been in his position for at least five years. Reid's FBI tech support managed to narrow down the list of possible suspects to less than fifty of the lawmakers in Austin, but that wasn't much help.

And that left Reid with one hope—Travis. But although Trav had made introductions and taken him to political gatherings, he seemed hesitant to answer Reid's questions without an adequate explanation. Maybe the real trouble between the two old friends stemmed less from ten years of noncontact than it did from something pertaining to that night so long ago. After all, didn't Reid remember that Trav had been nervous and jumpy before he'd left the house?

Or perhaps it came more from Reid's supposed treatment of Jill back then. Maybe Travis had bought his uncle's lies too. The same as Jill had so easily done.

Right now, Trav was still waiting for an answer. Reid had only asked about Jill as a way to warm her cousin up. Obviously, the ploy had backfired.

"I congratulated her on her engagement the other night," Reid managed at last. "And then yesterday when

I ran into her, she wasn't wearing the diamond ring. I
didn't want to seem too nosy. Do you know what happened?''

"What's it to you, old buddy? Maybe she's having the
ring sized. You lost the right to ask anything about Jill
when you jilted her the day of your wedding." Travis's
words were rough, but his eyes held an old echo of sympathy.

Reid knew he had to be careful. Although he couldn't
really believe his old friend could be involved, Travis's
name *was* on the list of fifty suspects. But his need for
Travis's help far outweighed any other consideration.

"Look, Trav. It's a long story and it happened a long
time ago. I'm not terribly comfortable going into the details but, believe me, I didn't leave voluntarily. Be a
friend and don't ask me to explain more."

Reid watched his old pal with the practiced eye of a
trained investigator. Travis hadn't flinched at Reid's par-
tial explanation. Perhaps Jill's father, Andrew, had told
Travis what had happened after Reid was knocked out.
That idea didn't exactly sit well with Reid. Surely Travis
would have said something more if he'd known the
whole story.

Reid couldn't take the time to inquire about personal
matters right this minute. His own puzzling past wasn't
the mystery he was currently working to solve. Later,
when he'd located his quarry, he vowed to come back
and question Travis further.

But that was later. Right now, Reid needed to make
peace with Travis. Whatever it took.

"You'll never know how sorry I am that I hurt Jill.
I'd have moved heaven and earth to keep that from happening. I still care enough not to want to see her hurt
again." Reid sighed and set his beer down on the counter.

"I was just curious to know if this jerk fiancé of hers took his ring back for some reason. And, if so, should I take the guy's head off, or what?"

Travis's grip tightened around his bottle. "Look, *you* weren't the one who spent hours, days…damn it…weeks having her cry on your shoulder. *You* weren't the one who watched over her for the last ten years, making sure nothing else bad touched her. She sure as hell doesn't need *you* now." He drained the bottle and hung his head.

"Aw, never mind. Just leave her alone, Sorrels. Bill Baldwin is the best thing to happen to her in her whole life. In eighteen months, he'll be governor of this great state, and if I have any influence over her, she'll be the first lady."

"Travis, I didn't mean…" Reid knew by the look in his friend's eyes that it was time to shut up and take his losses. Apparently, talking about Jill was not going to win him any points tonight.

"Yeah, okay," Reid mumbled. "Let me buy you another beer."

He hailed the bartender and indicated they'd have one more round. "Why don't you tell me about this Baldwin guy? What's he done that's so stellar?"

"For one thing, Bill Baldwin would never leave Jill…for any reason." Travis gave his friend a cutting look, then shook his head. "Sorry. That wasn't fair. I do believe you didn't want to hurt her, even though I'd like a better explanation of what really happened."

Travis hesitated, but when Reid didn't interrupt him, he went on. "Okay, forget it. Back to Baldwin. He's by far the best politician I've ever run across in my eight years in state government. Not only will he make a great governor, he'll be one of this century's greatest presidents. You mark my words."

Reid nodded but kept a questioning look in his eyes. Travis took the bait and continued his recitation of Bill's virtues.

"When he served in the legislature with me a few years ago, he formed one of the first committees to conduct talks with our neighbors to the south." Travis ran his hand down the wet, slick longneck and began picking at the paper label. "Now that Baldwin is attorney general, he holds regular discussions with the governors of our bordering states, including the states within Mexico. His contacts alone have saved us from many an international incident."

Travis went on for another half hour extolling the attributes of Bill Baldwin. Reid let him ramble, but something kept nagging at him. By the time Trav wound down and went home, Reid had a gut suspicion that Baldwin would make a good suspect. The man seemed to meet all the criteria even though he hadn't appeared on Operation Rock-A-Bye's "top fifty" list. Reid placed a call to his office for more intelligence about Baldwin while he thought more about Jill's current engagement.

Later, he headed back to his mother's ranch. Regardless of the consequences, and regardless of what it might cost him in self-respect, Reid figured he had to spend more time with Jill. She was the fastest way and best bet for getting close to his new suspect.

Not to mention the fact that he would delight in seeing to it that Jill Bennett didn't end up marrying the guy. Reid hadn't cared for Baldwin from the first minute they'd been introduced, standing there with his arm around Jill in all his slick glory. Baldwin obviously would do whatever it took to win politically. Maybe he'd found a way to add to his own political coffers—illegally—on the backs of stolen babies and heartbroken parents.

Reid refused to think that his own motives weren't totally pure...that he might be trying to deliberately cause Jill trouble and pain. After all, he was a better man than to hold that kind of grudge for all these years. He would never hurt her or her innocent son in any way. No, he vowed to try to keep both of them from being devastated.

But he had a job to do. He needed to bring down his suspect. Besides, it was her fiancé Baldwin that turned his gut inside out with all his phony macho bravado, not Jill. And it was Baldwin he was now determined to go after.

And damn it all, but the best way to spend time with Jill was to spend time with her son. He would really feel like a slimeball using Andy to get to Jill—to get to Baldwin. But if that's what it took to bring down the master criminal of an international baby-selling ring...so be it.

A few days later, Jill stood in the cool depths of the foaling barn and watched as Reid set up a small barrel and bale of hay in the middle of one of the pens. Andy followed close behind him, dancing in and out of his shadows and babbling endlessly about the rodeo.

In the whole ten days since Reid first showed up at the fund-raiser, she hadn't been able to think of much else but him. Well, that wasn't strictly true. She'd also thought a lot about her son.

She reflected about all the years she'd grieved over the fact that Andy had no father. Jill clearly remembered a time when she'd imagined what a wonderful father Reid would've made. But that was before he just up and disappeared, leaving her to raise their son alone.

Regardless of what she'd told her meddling mother,

Jill knew she would eventually have to tell both Reid and Andy the truth. It was the right thing to do. And in the long run, she'd really have no choice. One way or the other, they'd find out anyway—then *she'd* be the bad guy. Goodness knows, she never wanted to experience Andy's disdain—if she could possibly avoid it.

Right this minute, she could only hope time was on her side. Maybe, given a little time, they'd learn to respect one another, and she could find an easy way to tell them both the truth.

All she had to do was pray that Reid didn't question Andy too closely about how old he was in the meantime. Her son's age might be her biggest pitfall. She felt confident that Andy had no reason to mention his age. At least not until it was closer to his birthday, which was over eight months away. But her grace period was perilous at best.

Soon. She needed to find a way to tell them—soon.

It didn't matter if Reid would be furious that she'd never told him about his son. She'd been plenty furious at him for leaving her almost at the altar. But it did matter what Andy thought. She didn't want her baby's life to be ruined by hate for a father who'd never been around— or hate for a mother who'd never told him the truth.

She looked out into the sunshine as Reid bent on one knee in the dust, explaining the finer points of knot tying to Andy. Their two heads leaned together in serious discussion. Jill mused about the differences between the man and his son.

Of course, their similarities were clearly visible. The dark, smoky eyes. The lean, wide-shouldered build. The big feet that always managed to be where they shouldn't be.

But it was the differences that captured Jill's attention.

Reid's work hat was pulled low on his forehead, covering his chestnut-colored hair. Andy wore no hat in the bright sunshine and his black curls shone with radiant highlights. As her child concentrated on the lesson, the tip of his tongue snuck out from the corner of his mouth, exactly the way hers always did when she was deep in thought.

Andy was definitely an eclectic combination of both his mother's and father's genes. That fact had given her some comfort when she'd thought about Andy spending time with his father. She'd figured Reid wouldn't be able to see his own eyes reflected in his son's because her family's features, so strong in her child, would shroud their true relationship.

But deep down, Jill knew the day of reckoning was coming. Somehow, one of the two of them would learn the facts. She wanted to find a way to ease them both into the truth first. They needed to learn to like each other, maybe to become friends before they had to face down their reality.

That was the real reason she'd agreed to letting them spend this time together. It definitely was *not* because she wanted to spend more time with Reid.

No way was she interested in the man anymore. Just because her body jolted every time he stood within three feet of her. Just because the sheer pleasure of looking at him made her relive the savage, raw passions they'd shared with glittering intensity. None of that meant anything today.

The things she'd been experiencing were strictly lustful memories. But she knew she could conquer those baser emotions if she put her mind to it. At this moment, her son was the most important consideration.

"Hi, Mom." Andy had spotted her and was waving. "Come on over here."

Too late to duck, Jill stepped out into the sunshine and strode over to them. "How's the lesson going?"

Reid stood, placed his hands on his narrow hips and eyed her with a purposeful gleam. His biceps and chest muscles rippled under his navy blue T-shirt as he fisted his hands. He smiled at her with the same charmingly crooked smile she always remembered, while she swallowed hard and tried to concentrate on her son.

Andy moved toward her, then bounced back to pick up the lasso he'd dropped.

"Great, Mom." Andy's body fairly shimmered with enthusiasm as he pulled the rope through his fingers. "Mr. Sorrels is teaching me all his secrets."

"That's wonderful, sweetheart." Jill placed a hand on her son's shoulder in a futile effort to keep him still.

Her hand slipped over his rough, denim shirt as Andy spun to talk to Reid. "Tell her what you just told me." He ran to Reid's side and tugged on his shirtsleeve. "Tell Mom, Mr. Sorrels."

"Andy, for goodness' sake, calm down." Jill moved closer to the man and boy in order to get a firm grip on her son—then wished she hadn't.

Up this close, she got a whiff of Reid's aftershave. Citrusy and musky all at the same time, the smell of him threatened to open forbidden doors in her heart. Doors she'd closed off years ago in order to protect herself. Her knees started to shake and she made a quick grab for Andy's shoulders to help her keep her balance.

Reid grinned down at Andy. "Take it easy, kid. We'll get everything said that needs to be said. All things happen in their own time."

His gaze traveled up past Andy's forehead and cen-

tered about the middle of Jill's chest, making her wish
she'd worn a bulky sweatshirt instead of this thin T-shirt.
The look on Reid's face darkened as he took the time to
dwell on her body before he finally settled on her red-
dening face.

"Jill." He took off his hat while his eyes never left
hers. "I didn't think you were coming out to the ranch
today. Weren't you supposed to be in court?"

Heat flared inside her as she clung to her son and at
the same time kept her shoulders back and her spine
straight. She wouldn't let Reid see that he could get to
her. She refused to be so...so... Well, she just refused,
period.

"The case settled at the last minute." Her voice
sounded reedy and too high to her ears.

She gladly turned her attention to Andy. "Son, have
you been good for Mr. Sorrels like we talked about?"

Andy nodded so hard she worried that he might break
something. "Yes'um. But wait'll you hear what he said."
Andy pulled a shoulder free from his mother's grip.

Reid chuckled softly and fingered the hat in his hand.
"I was just telling Andy here that he has a natural way
with a rope. It also seems like he might've been born to
the saddle. He'll make a rodeo star someday, for sure."

Jill took a deep breath. She had no intention of talking
about what her son had been born to do. Not yet.

Reid must've caught her hesitation. His expression
hardened and he furrowed his brow as he studied her.

"You're not going to make a fuss about him trying his
hand at an event are you? He won't go until he's ready.
I promise you that." Reid's dark look threatened to strip
bare every one of her secrets.

She dropped her hands to her side. "Oh no. It's not
that at all."

Great. She'd just denied a reasonable explanation that might've covered for her real problem—at least for a little while. Now she was left with no excuse. No defense.

Luckily for her, right then Andy's stomach growled loudly enough to be heard in two counties. Saved.

She gathered all her motherly instincts and turned to her son. "It's lunchtime, Andy. Better head on up to the house and see what Nana has cooking."

"Aw, Mom."

She watched her son battle between his hunger and the desire to continue with his favorite pastime. Hunger won. Andy grabbed Reid's huge hand with his small one, and Jill had to stifle a sigh, wishing for things that couldn't be.

"Come on, Mr. Sorrels. Let's go get something to eat."

When he looked up at Reid, Jill's heart thudded in her chest. Her son's gaze held such trust, such worship and longing that she wondered if allowing the two time together might become one of the worst mistakes of her life.

What if Andy grew to love the man? What if after he knew the truth, Reid didn't want to be tied down with a son? Would he disappear from Andy's life, leaving their son with only broken dreams—the same way he'd left her?

Suddenly everything she'd done so far seemed all wrong.

"I'm sure Mr. Sorrels is too busy to spend any more time with you today, son. You go on up to the house. I need to talk to Reid for a few minutes, then I'll be up to join you."

"But..." Andy whined.

"You do as your mother says, boy," Reid urged. "We

can work on your roping another day. The rodeo isn't going to shut down. It'll still be there when you get ready for it.''

Reid had been fascinated by the mix of emotions he'd observed on Jill's face. The last time he'd seen her, he'd wondered if she had something to hide. Now he was sure she did.

Only now, Reid feared she was not only hiding something from him but hiding something from her son as well. Perhaps she was afraid to tell Andy about her engagement. Maybe Baldwin didn't really care much for the boy.

That would be one more reason to see to it that Jill broke off the relationship. Reid decided to make sure that happened. He decided to use whatever means necessary to keep them apart permanently. After all, having to tell one more lie to her or anyone else wouldn't be the end of the world.

"Go to the house, Andy," Jill demanded in that motherly tone that made every young boy cringe.

"Yes'um." He swung around and shuffled off reluctantly.

Restless, Reid worked his jaw. He ached inside every time he thought back to ten years ago. Every time he got close to what he'd lost.

He hadn't wanted to put that much of an emotional investment into this mission for Operation Rock-A-Bye, but it was already too late to stop. Much too late.

Jill turned to look at him. In the sunshine, her eyes were the color of a clear West Texas sky at midday. How often had he dreamed of seeing her gazing up at him in just this way? How often had he longed for the comfort of her lithe body nestled in his arms, the sweet agony of her kiss against his lips?

He shook off the images. This was undercover work. Nothing more. Putting on his hat and taking her by the arm, he ambled in the direction of his truck, wondering what she had to say. Wondering if he could keep his hands to himself and wondering if he could keep the memories locked inside his professional outer shell long enough to complete his mission.

Jill silently walked beside him. They made it through the foaling barn without saying a word.

"Reid, I..." she began.

"Jill, I..." he said at the same time.

Together, they laughed at their own nervousness. How strange to be so self-conscious with her. There was a time when the two of them had melded into one being. They'd been as close as two separate entities could be without losing their own identities.

Now... Now he wasn't sure he'd ever really known her. But he was determined not to let old memories stop him.

"You go first," she chuckled.

At the barn's far door, he hesitated before they stepped back out into the sun. "Jill, I need a friend." He took her hand in his, felt the electricity but held on. "My life is so messed up. I really appreciate you letting me help Andy. It's mending my spirits. But I also want to spend a little time with you. I want to be your friend as well as Andy's. I need someone to talk to."

She stared at him as if he were a perfect stranger.

"We used to be able to talk." He let a pleading tone seep into his voice, knowing she'd never resist an injured soul—just like she'd never been able to resist taking in sick strays as a girl.

"A lot of things have changed, Reid."

Steel words, but the softness he remembered was there

in her eyes and in the tone of her voice. "Yes they have. But some things will never..."

"Miz Bennett!" One of the ranch hands flew around the corner of the barn, his face contorted and his breath ragged.

"Miz Bennett, come quick!" The man gulped in air and grabbed Jill's arm.

"What is it? What's wrong?" she cried. "Has something happened to Mother?"

He shook his head violently. "It's your boy. He..." The man fought for his voice. "He's fallen into the pen. Oh God, ma'am. He's in with Ol' Pete."

# Four

If Jill had been capable of rational thought, she'd have wondered how a person could manage to go the two hundred feet or so from the foaling barn to the breeding pens without remembering having taken even one step. But suddenly she was facing chaos and horror as she stumbled into the heat and brilliant sunshine of the open yard.

When she'd stumbled, Reid grabbed her around the waist, steadying her for a second with his quiet, reassuring presence. But not for long. He stepped away and beat her to the wooden fencing separating them from her precious son—and from the huge, black-hided animal pawing the ground and snorting in the wind a few yards away.

She fought for breath as she reached the fence and tried to take in everything. Her brain was going in slow motion, while the world seemed brighter and more surreal somehow. She desperately tried to assimilate the scene before her. This wasn't a nightmare. This wasn't a movie.

That was Andy lying there so still and quiet just a few feet inside the fence rails in the dust. *Oh my God!*

Without missing a beat she climbed up the rails and prepared herself to jump over. He was hurt—in danger— and she had to get to her son.

Several strange arms reached for her, hauling her back to the ground with a shattering thud.

"You can't go in there, ma'am." One of her mother's ranch hands was screaming as he held her back.

"Let go of me," she wailed in frustration.

From the rear of the pen, a couple more of the men were making a racket, yelling, screaming and waving their arms at the confused and increasingly agitated beast. They were trying to take the bull's attention from the boy who lay silently a couple of feet away in a heap of rumpled clothes and a cloud of dust.

"Get him out of there!" Jill cried.

"We have to get the bull backed into the chute first, ma'am." The ranch hand with a tight grip on her arms screamed over the riotous noise. "If anyone goes in there now, we'll just end up with two dead people on our hands."

What had he said? Two...*dead*...people.

"Noooooo." Impossible. Not her son. Not Andy.

Her eyes teared over, blearing her vision and infuriating her. She needed all her strength and a clear head to get her boy out of this disaster.

Through the wet haze of anger and fear, Jill saw a movement from the far corner of the pen. Reid? Yes. He'd thrown a large bale of hay into the corner of the bull's pen and jumped in after it.

A cry of protest arose from the various men who

ringed the pen and the man holding her let her go to join them.

"Get out of there. You're aggravating him," someone hollered.

"Quiet!" Reid spoke in the most commanding voice Jill had ever heard.

If he'd been a general and all the men his soldiers, he couldn't have made more of an impression on everyone concerned. Including the bull.

Nothing moved. For one instant, silence filled the air.

Reid was the first to make a move. He stepped around the hay and stood there, quietly appraising the bull.

"Hey, Pete," he finally said. "You upset with us?"

The bull stared at the man in his pen, but the soothing words seemed to temporarily paralyze him.

"Now I know this isn't home, and these old boys aren't your regular friends. But they don't mean you any harm."

From behind his back, Reid pulled a length of rope. He dangled it through his hands while the bull watched in a fascinated stupor.

Reid took a couple of steps toward the bull, putting himself between the mighty animal and the boy. "It's time to calm down now, Pete. Are you hungry?"

He picked up a handful of the hay and waved it at the bull's face. "This isn't your usual gourmet feed, but maybe you'd like to try a bite?"

The bull lowered his head and snorted a couple of times. The animal actually seemed to know the sound of Reid's voice.

Reid used his booted toe to push the broken bale of hay in the direction of the chute, used mainly to move the bull into his private enclosure. "Come on, Pete," he murmured.

Jill was stunned to see the gigantic beast move slowly toward Reid and the hay—and away from Andy's body. At the thought, she turned to inspect her son. He was so still. She couldn't even be sure that he was breathing.

Things were going way too slow. She needed to get her son out of the pen and away from the danger—immediately.

All of the ranch hands were silently staring at Reid and the bull at the far end of the pen. Jill figured with everyone's attention elsewhere, she'd have a perfect opportunity to go for Andy.

Silently, stealthily, she crawled under the bottom rail of the wooden fence nearest her son. No one seemed to notice or pay her any attention. Including, thank God, the bull.

Reid's actions were so mesmerizing, she was on her hands and knees at Andy's side before anyone saw her.

She had only a split second to discover that Andy was, indeed, still breathing, before a ranch hand cried out in shock at her position.

"Hey, you shouldn't be in there!" he shouted.

Suddenly everyone's attention became focused on her and the lifeless body lying beside her. The bull made a strangled noise in his throat and then roared his disapproval, pawing the ground and bucking his back.

Instantaneously, Jill pulled Andy into her arms and jumped to her feet. Her child was a heavy load, but she knew she could get him to the fence by herself. She took the four or five steps, her feet barely touching the ground.

At the fence she had time to blink once, wondering how on earth she would get herself and her son over or under in a hurry. Instead, they were both whisked up by a pair of muscular arms and thrown unceremoniously over the top. Jill landed, her body covering Andy on the other side. Shifting to her hands and knees in a desperate effort to move off of him, she tried, at the same time, to find out how close the bull might be by now.

She could hear the sound of heavy, thundering hooves that seemed to be right above her head. Looking up through a haze of dust and a mass of her own curls that had flopped into her face, Jill saw Reid vault over the fence—just in time to miss Ol' Pete's furious charge.

Almost.

Pete caught Reid's right leg at the ankle, smashing it into one of the posts and nearly coming through the fence on top of them all. Fortunately, the fence held and Reid, dragging his leg up and over the highest rail, tumbled to the ground, landing next to Jill with a thud.

Reid winched as the emergency room doctor gingerly tightened the bandage around his right foot. The woman doctor was smiling at him while she gave him a lecture on how to care for a sprained ankle. He didn't need any lecture on his health. He'd spent so many months in the hospital after being left for dead ten years ago that he knew the name of every muscle and bone in the human body, along with the required treatment for every injury known to affect them. After all, he wasn't called the "master of wheelchair racing" for nothing.

The doctor smiled at him again as she wrote on a prescription pad. At this late hour, he didn't feel much like smiling. Not since this afternoon when he'd been forced to relinquish his hold on Jill as one of the ranch hands helped her into the back of the Suburban to ride to the hospital with her son. Until then, he'd kept up a steady, calm front.

Reid knew his own injury was minor—a slight hindrance for a couple of weeks, nothing more. But he wasn't so positive about Andy. After he'd thrown the mother and child over the fence and hoisted himself away from the bull, he'd whisked the two of them into the ranch house as fast as he could manage with his injured ankle.

Andy had moaned low in his throat as he'd placed the boy down on the living room couch to await a ride to the hospital. So he knew the child still lived, but obviously he had a head injury, and there was no way of telling how bad that might be without the equipment and expertise at the regional hospital.

Frustration gnawed at him. Since arriving at the emergency room, he couldn't get anyone to tell him anything about Andy's condition. He couldn't even manage to get out of emergency long enough to push someone in administration for the information he desired. He had a few contacts here that he could manipulate, but before trying that route he'd been forced into letting them treat his own injury.

So far, he'd been x-rayed, prodded, packed in ice and now wrapped. His patience disappeared with the pain.

"You Reid Sorrels?" A burly man in a white uniform stuck his head inside the closed curtain surrounding Reid and the lady doctor.

"What?" Reid was startled out of his personal fog. "Yeah, I'm Sorrels.... Why?"

"There's a woman upstairs that's concerned about you. She asked me to check up."

Only one woman could be in this hospital that might have reason to ask about his welfare. Jill.

"Where is she?" Reid eased off the table and tested the strength of the tightly wrapped bandage.

"Hold your horses," the doctor snapped. "Let me at

least get you a wheelchair before you go gallivanting off
around the hospital corridors.''

"No, thanks." Reid reached for his socks. "Can you
hand me my one remaining boot, please?"

The doctor turned to the closet as the man at the curtain shifted impatiently. "So whatta you want me to tell
her, bud? I gotta be getting back," he grumbled.

"I don't want you to tell her anything. I'll tell her.
You just show me where she is," Reid demanded as he
slipped on his socks.

The doctor handed him a rather dusty but perfectly
intact lizard-skin boot. One. For the left foot.

"Sorry we had to cut the other one off you," she said.
"I don't suppose you'll be able to replace one boot."

He shook his head as an answer. It didn't matter. The
boots weren't new. They'd been new ten years ago. For
all this time they'd sat in his mother's house, waiting for
him to need them again. It'd been difficult to put them
on without facing his memories. A new pair would be
easier to live with, anyhow.

Reid reluctantly accepted the crutches the doctor insisted he use. Awkwardly, he followed the man, who'd
turned out to be an X-ray technician, into the elevator
and up the three flights to pediatrics.

Following the technician's instructions, he rounded a
corner heading for Andy's room. Because he was so focused on relearning how to use crutches, he nearly
rammed into Jill's back as she stood leaning against a
wall talking quietly on a pay phone. She was engrossed
in her conversation and missed his clumsy intrusion.

He stopped, but didn't have the wherewithal or the
desire to back up and give her the privacy he knew she
deserved. Shamelessly, he quieted his breathing in an at-
tempt to overhear her side of the call.

"Yes, I know how important this trip is," she said in a hushed tone. "But I thought maybe Andy was important, too."

The hallways were deserted this time of night, the lights lowered to a twilight hue. Jill's shoulders were slumped with fatigue, her hair a mass of tangled curls. Reid's fingers itched to smooth the wayward strands back off her face. But he stood still and let her finish.

"Of course I realize you need to make the meeting in order to ensure our future." She listened silently, then spoke through clenched teeth. "Right Bill, I know that means Andy's future too. But..."

She straightened her spine and stepped away from the wall, still not aware of Reid's presence. "It's just that you meet with the Mexican governors of Neuvo Leon and Coahuila nearly every month. I thought this one time you could assign someone else to take your place."

In the dim light, Reid saw her silently shake her head in an apparent response to what was being said to her. "Never mind. I understand," she said soberly. "I'll talk to you in a couple of days."

Jill lowered the phone to its cradle, heaved a heavy sigh and rolled her shoulders. He felt an unexpected surge of tenderness toward her, as if he had every right to pull her into his arms and comfort her.

He reached out to touch her arm. "Jill," he whispered.

She whirled around, surprised by the sound of his voice. "Oh, Reid. There you are. Are you all right?"

She stared down at the crutches and his one stocking-clad foot and shook her head. "Oh, dear."

Stepping quickly to his side, she studied his face as if doing so would reassure her that everything was going to be okay. Tears welled in her eyes, making them darken to a deep, blue-velvet color.

"I'm really fine, Jill. It's just a little sprain. How's Andy?"

He'd deliberately spoken in a hushed but commanding tone. He sensed she needed a quiet, steady hand right now, and that was one thing he could provide.

In the shadows of the hall, he saw her bite her lip as if unsure of her answer or unsure of what to say to him. The hesitant gesture was so unlike the new, confident Jill that he flashed back to the vulnerable, innocent girl she'd been when they'd first found love. He'd never stopped thinking about her that way. Not really.

In his mind, he pictured that bottom lip the way it was back then. Swollen and moist from his kisses or quivering with anticipation as his hands moved across her body's curves. He remembered the taste of those lips—hot, sweet and silky. Instantly, he needed to taste them again. To feel her smooth, honeyed mouth underneath his own once more.

As if she'd read his desires, she took a step back. "I'm not sure… How Andy is doing, I mean." She took another step back, putting distance between them and between him and his memories. "The doctors say he has a concussion. A mild one. But they're concerned because he seems so groggy still."

"What are they doing for him?" He swung his crutch, taking a hesitant step in a direction he thought sure would lead to Andy's room.

"Nothing. They say we just have to wait. The nurses have been rousing him every hour, looking in his eyes, that sort of thing. I guess they plan on doing that all night."

He could see the purple smudges under her eyes now. The deep fatigue that this day had caused was clearly visible even in the dim light. Confused by the ache inside him at the reminder of her pain, he turned away from the sight and fumbled with the crutches as she moved ahead of him into Andy's room.

As his eyes adjusted to the dim lighting in the room, Reid was stunned at the sight of the boy lying asleep in the hospital bed. Andy looked so small. Reid had thought of him as a big, strapping kid—healthy and so alive. Now he looked like the little boy of six or seven that he really was. The child in front of him was sunken into the huge bed, quiet and...still. Too still.

A skyrocketing feeling of protective guardianship coursed through him for the second time in the last five minutes. He'd never felt anything like this before. This deep, irrational possessiveness toward both the woman and child. It was almost like they were his to take care of and worry about.

Of course, that was nonsense. Perhaps this urge came from his years as a special agent in charge, totally in control of his agents' welfare. But it really didn't feel quite the same, he decided.

A nurse walked into Andy's room, slowing when she realized Reid and Jill were hovering over his bed.

"Ms. Bennett? I'm taking over your son's care for the third shift. I have orders to sit with him for a few hours."

The nurse scrutinized Jill's face, then added. "Why don't you go on home and get some rest? I'll be here, and if anything changes, I'll call you back immediately."

Jill shook her head. "You're as bad as my mother. She's been calling all night, wanting me to come home. I'm not leaving. I'm fine."

"Ma'am, the hospital is full, we don't have any extra beds. You look like you're about ready to fall down right here. Please go home." The nurse turned to Reid as if he could help convince the stubborn mother.

Jill sighed deeply. She knew she was exhausted, but she feared if she tried to sleep now, all the emotions of the last twelve hours would come pouring out to swamp her.

"Is there a couch somewhere where she can lie down?" Reid's look was compassionate—and something more. But Jill was too tired to ferret out what was going on with him.

The nurse looked thoughtful for a second. "Well, yes. Since this is the pediatrics wing, we have a playroom and waiting room combination that should be empty at this hour. I can't recommend it for any quality sleep, but if you refuse to go home, it's down at the far end of the hall to your left."

Jill was stuck between needing to sit down and not wanting to leave her son's side for one instant. Reid made the decision for her. He took her arm and urged her to move out the door while he followed behind with his crutches.

"Come on," he said. "I'll sit with you so you won't be alone."

She was grateful to Reid for being there when she needed a friend. At the stray thought, she suddenly remembered what he'd been talking about right before Andy fell into the bull's pen and knocked himself out. He'd said he needed a friend to talk to.

She decided maybe whatever he'd wanted to say would take her mind off Andy for a little while. Slowly strolling toward the darkened and peaceful waiting room, she stayed close to Reid as he inched his way down the slick hall.

"Jill, quit pacing and come sit down." Reid patted the space on the plastic covered couch next to him.

She'd had every intention of resting when they'd first entered the waiting room. But after settling Reid down and storing his crutches, she'd decided he was probably hungry since he hadn't eaten all day. She found an alcove nearby with food and drink machines and brought him a couple packages of cheese crackers and a hot coffee.

Not much of a supper she knew, but better than nothing at this point. Guilt for getting him hurt in the first place was beginning to nag at her conscience. So far, she and Andy had caused him nothing but trouble.

Nervous energy and pent up anxiety kept her standing as Reid choked down a few of the crackers and gulped a bit of the steaming coffee. He raised one eyebrow.

"I thought we came in here so you could rest." His voice suddenly took on that same commanding quality it had in Pete's pen this afternoon. "Sit."

She plopped down next to him and squeezed her eyes shut. Visions of Andy lying facedown in the dust filled her mind.

Reid put a warm hand on her arm and immediately blood rushed not only to that spot but also to other parts of her that didn't need awakening at the moment. She was too vulnerable right now.

He must have felt it too, because he removed his hand, leaving her cold and filled once more with the caution and fear that had been her prison for the last ten years. She shivered involuntarily.

"You're cold." Reid shifted, putting an arm around her shoulders and pulling her close.

Warm and inviting, the smell of real male and hot coffee was too comfortable—too inviting. She couldn't deal with this—with Reid—tonight.

She started to shake, waves of nervous tension crashing in around her. The defenses she'd placed around her heart all day to stay strong for Andy began to crumble. Here in Reid's arms was a safe haven.

No, safe was not the word for Reid's arms. She'd thought she'd been safe there once, a long time ago. Now they were inviting, strong, and...sexy as all get out, but she would be far from safe in his embrace.

She would never be completely safe again. Not like she'd dreamed about as a girl, anyway.

Older and much wiser, she knew that she must stand on her own two feet and be the solid foundation for herself and her child. But, oh, the way he was looking at her was so compelling—so sweet and understanding.

Assailed by needs and rocked by the fears and horrors of the long day looming back to devil her, Jill tried to stem the tears suddenly building up behind her eyes. She bit down hard on her bottom lip and sniffed with the losing battle.

"Don't," Reid warned quietly. His soft words and stirring presence made the tears flow even stronger.

"Ah, hell." He reached out, pulling her tighter to his chest and locking his arms around her back. "It'll be all right, sweetheart. I'm here. Everything will be all right."

# Five

Jill melted into Reid's body like warm butter. The feel of her delicious curves pressed against him and her obvious struggle to stem the tears made him lose control. He forgot the years and the pain that separated them. Forgot that he had to use her and Andy to get his suspect. Forgot they were in a public place.

"Damn, Jill. Don't cry." He pressed a kiss into her hair, wanting to sooth her with tenderness and strength.

She cried all the harder at his caress.

"Please don't," he begged, as he moved his lips to her delicate earlobe.

She sobbed openly, and he skimmed his mouth over her jawline, wet with salty tears. His heart contracted at the taste of those tears.

Without thinking, he lightly cruised his mouth over hers, silencing her sobs in the only way he could. He wanted her to know he was sorry for her pain, that he'd never let anything hurt her or Andy again. When he brushed those inviting lips with his own, he felt her settle against him, quieting as she began to accept the comfort he gave.

The emergence of desire took him by surprise. The soft brushing of lips became hungry and desperately needy. He slanted his mouth over hers and deepened the kiss. Putting all the pent-up wants and dreams of ten years into his burning caress, he tried to give her all his strength.

Jill slid her arms around his neck and clung to him. Her sobs turned into mewing little moans. She opened for him, and he feasted on her wet warmth and inviting tongue.

Ten years disappeared. He was home. Where he belonged.

Fisting his hands in her hair, he let the silky strands float against his palms, losing himself in the sensuous sensations. Like the first food after a long fast, he consumed her.

He inhaled her womanly scent, moved his hands to her arms and rubbed lightly over the velvety skin there. He wanted her essence to surround him, wanted to lose himself ever deeper into her being.

Reid pulled her into his lap, eager to let her feel what she'd done to him. Jill was way ahead of him. She ground her bottom into his arousal, making it thicken and lengthen even more. She groaned as he slid his hands around her ribcage and softly skimmed them over her breasts.

Perfect. He dipped his tongue into her sweetness once again and fell into his memories. Like an echo off a steep canyon wall, she tasted like the promises of forever and trust—in the same ways she always had. She was everything he remembered, and more.

He swallowed a tortured groan, forgetting all the heartache of the past. Forgetting everything but the here and now—the fire racing through his veins. Lightly, he ran his tongue over her moist lips in slow, tender passes, feeding the flames between them. The realities of who they were and where they were slipped away, leaving raw passion and a shameless, wanton need to possess.

Reid sucked her deep into his mouth, desperate to satisfy her every desire—assailed by the sudden wildfire spreading across his body with abandon. His soul remembered this place as a shelter of positive energy, a haven for the body and a sacred closet for the spirit.

Somehow, out of his haze of desire and over their heavy breathing, Reid heard footsteps clicking against the linoleum down the hallway. He jerked his head away from the honey of her lips and looked over her shoulder to find the source of the noise.

Jill buried her face in his shoulder and moaned.

Two nurses, apparently on break, whispered to each other as they passed the waiting room and headed for the alcove containing the food and drink machines. When Reid finally managed to think and breathe again, he gently pushed Jill back from his chest so he could talk to her.

The bruised look of her swollen lips assaulted his senses. Wordlessly berating himself for the loss of control, he swore he should've kept his damn hands to himself.

Slowly, Jill opened her midnight eyes and gazed at him with heavy-lidded, undisguised desire. Oh, man.

Reid had done a lot of underhanded things in the name of justice over the last ten years, but he'd never moved in on a woman that belonged to someone else. And Jill was apparently still engaged. For now.

"That shouldn't have happened," he managed with an unsteady rasp.

He let his fingers smooth away a dark curl that had matted itself to her cheek—because he really had no choice. Also without permission, his wayward thumbs rubbed lightly under her eyes, drying leftover tears. But he quickly decided he couldn't look at the creamy-white skin on her cheeks, touch that silkiness, or gaze into the depths of those dreamy eyes for one more second.

He wrapped his arms around her tightly and used his palm to press her head back against his shoulder. "Sleep, Jill. We'll talk later."

The next two days went by in a whirl for Jill. Andy was released from the hospital when, by the afternoon following the incident with the bull, he'd been as alert and clear-eyed as normal.

His doctor shook his head with a chuckle and said, "I wish we could all bounce back as fast as kids do."

Her mom came in the SUV, complete with her normal histrionics, and drove them back to the ranch.

Jill was amazed that although Reid hadn't left her side in over twenty-four hours, they'd never had an opportunity for the conversation that was, by now, well overdue. He was concerned and giving, exactly like the husband and father she'd imagined he could've been. And not at all like the low-down scum that had left her for another woman the day of their wedding—the way she'd thought of him ever since.

She'd been so concerned about Andy's welfare that she'd practically forgotten Reid's request for her friendship. But she hadn't forgotten the late-night kiss. Probably she never would.

Jill insisted that Reid recuperate from his sprained ankle at her mother's ranch rather than trying to go back to his own mother's house. They had plenty of room and her mother kept a ton of household help on the payroll, unlike Reid's mother, who managed to get by alone.

Jill felt she owed him something for helping to save Andy. Secretly, she was also curious to find out what he might have to say about the surprise kiss they'd shared. With no idea at all what to think about the seductive desire and deep need that kiss had stirred, she was hoping maybe Reid could make some sense out of it.

Perhaps if they talked civilly, the mystery and the urgent wanting would be cleared away. She had to continue with her life and stop walking around in a fog of confusion.

Andy needed her.

She stood in the late afternoon shadows on her mother's flagstone patio and gave a quick backward glance to her childhood home. It was such an odd mixture of all things Texan—and—the snobbish, Old South. Stucco and brick in varying shades of sand and cedar spoke to a heritage of the Old West. Huge arches with stately cactus standing over beds of wildflowers in a profusion of yellow and orange hues seemed somehow to be a mixture of both east and west. While this patio with its manicured grass and magnolia trees felt like a typical Louisiana plantation.

Jill felt she was also a curious mixture of two heritages. Her father's family, Texans for four generations, had sent their two boys to law school in Houston. Her mother's family, Shreveport gentry who'd lost their land, sent their only daughter to school in Houston to find a rich oilman to marry.

Love brought the two sides together.

If Jill hadn't come along when she did, her mother's family might've disowned their daughter forever. As it was, Jill's maternal grandparents only managed to tolerate her father—until he began making money and contributing to their retirement. In the last few years of his life, Jill's father had come into his own, making his in-laws proud—and rich.

Jill turned to face the setting sun and gazed down the little incline to the many out-barns and cattle pens in the distance. She knew beyond them, past acres of grazing pastures, lay the thickets of cedar and pines surrounding Long Lake, one of the many sapphire-colored lakes that blessed the Austin vicinity.

As suffocating and boring as she'd always found the ranch, she loved this land. The look and the feel of it soothed her soul. Perhaps Andy would one day want to make the place his home.

That would've pleased her father no end, Jill silently smiled to herself. He'd bought this place when she was a child because it had been his dream to own a Texas-size ranch.

When he died, Andrew Bennett left his share of the legal firm entirely to his brother, whose son, her cousin Trav, now ran it. A few years later, Travis took Jill into the firm when she'd passed the bar, giving her a job and a new lease on life.

But it was her mother that had turned their rural homestead into a real working cattle ranch. As pampered and prone to overreacting as she was, Caroline Bennett turned out to be a terrific businesswoman. When her husband left her with only a small amount of insurance, she turned a few head of cattle and ten thousand acres of land into a showplace.

Both of her parents had wanted the place to become a family heritage. The Double B Ranch—the Bennett Place.

Reid and Andy appeared from the shadowed depths of the nearest barn. At the mere sight of the man, her pulse started hammering and she ran a hand through her unruly hair.

Father and son moved closer, at a tortuously slow gait, Reid leaning on Andy's shoulder for added support. With his other arm, Reid worked a cane like an old master. Meanwhile, Andy gazed up at him in a rapt, hero-worshiping, way.

Jill knew just how he felt. With Reid's shirtsleeves rolled halfway up—displaying arms corded with muscles—and his jeans riding low on his washboard-flat belly, the man was too good to be true.

She flashed back to the other night when, for a few minutes, those tanned, sinewy arms felt strong and solid and safe—the way she dreamed about for her whole life. Today, he wore a black stretchy shirt and black Stetson that shadowed his eyes. Walking beside Andy, he looked big and tough and just a little bit dangerous—and a whole lot more like a cowboy than the desk-bound bureaucrat he claimed to be.

"Hey, Mom!" Andy yelled, when he looked up and saw her standing there. "Look how good Reid can walk on his hurt ankle now."

Jill smiled at her son's grammar, but knew mothers everywhere would disown her if she didn't correct him when he made a mistake. "It's 'how *well'*…"

Whoa. Had he said *Reid?* "Andy, I don't think you

should address Mr. Sorrels as 'Reid.' It sounds disrespectful." *And perhaps dangerous for keeping secrets.*

"Oh, that's okay. He said I could. He said since we've become friends, that it's what friends do."

Jill bit down on her lip. That they should be friends was what she wanted, wasn't it? So why, when they'd done just that, did she wonder if the whole idea was a mistake? Between her growing guilt for not telling them the truth immediately and her worry over Reid asking Andy his age, her nerves were frayed.

She looked up at Reid and found her answers at once. The way he was looking at her made her feel like a coward. When he and Andy discovered the truth about each other, it would be better if they were friends. But when Reid did find out, it would be the end of any friendship chances she might've had with him. He would be furious with her, and perhaps rightly so.

On second thought, how selfish could she be, for heaven's sake?

The two of them deserved to know about each other. Besides, Jill wasn't sure exactly what kind of relationship she really wanted with Reid, anyway. She'd told herself when he'd mentioned a friendship, that maybe they could put the past behind them and become something close to that.

The thought now seemed ridiculous. Every time they were within two feet of one another, the intoxicating pull of sexual lust between them left very little room to build a platonic relationship. Like right now, for instance.

His gaze burned inside, making her feel beads of sweat forming in all her hidden, dark places. A tug deep in her belly drew her attention to the fact that she was already wet at the juncture of her thighs and squirming internally at his nearness. When just a glance from the man could do that to her, Jill knew they could never be just friends.

There was too much between them. Too much hurt. Too much guilt. Sex would only compound the problems.

"Jill?" Reid's gaze suddenly changed to confusion and his shoulders tensed with concern. "Where'd you go there, sweetheart?" he probed.

She glanced around, wondering what had happened while she was so lost in thought.

Reid finally chortled at her dazed look. "Andy was asking you a question."

She looked down at her son's earnest expression and her heart sank. What would he think when he learned the truth?

"Mo...ooom." When he saw he finally had her attention, Andy repeated his question. "If Reid's ankle is good enough, he wants us all to go to the rodeo this weekend. Can we, puleeease?"

"Sure, honey." Jill answered with her heart's desire before she had a chance to consider the ramifications...or her other obligations.

"Yippee! I'm going to the rodeo." Andy was jumping and pumping his fist in the air.

"Uh. Wait a minute, son." Oh, how Jill hated to backtrack and disappoint her son. "I forgot that I promised Mr. Baldwin we'd go with him to the regatta this weekend. You remember. We talked about it a few days ago."

She could barely believe that she'd totally forgotten about Bill. She hadn't given him even a blink of a thought since they'd returned to the ranch from the hospital.

As if this whole situation wasn't complicated enough, Jill wondered what Bill would think when he found out that Reid was Andy's father. Not to mention what he'd say when he realized she hadn't been married when Andy was born. Appearances were paramount in any political campaign.

"Aw, Mom," Andy whined. "Do we have to?"

He turned to Reid for support, clearly hoping for divine intervention. "You talk to her, sir. You can make her say yes. She really likes you. I can tell."

"Is it really so important, Jill?" Reid asked, turning his dark, intense eyes to her. "I hate to see the boy disappointed. Can't you put Baldwin off this time?"

Despite suddenly wanting—no needing—to do whatever it took to make Reid happy, she forced herself to shake her head. "It's politics. The governor and many of the legislators will be there. The regatta's a fundraiser...and in memoriam to one of Bill's biggest contributors."

A series of strange looks spun through Reid's eyes. He appeared to be a man warring within himself. After a brief period of silence, he clenched his jaw and the darkest of those expressions moved over his face, setting his features into a hard cast.

"Perhaps we could arrange both." Reid's words were caring, compromising and clever, and not at all scary.

"We could all go to the regatta in the afternoon, then I'd drive us to the rodeo straight from there. Do you think Baldwin would mind if I tagged along to this fundraiser?"

After agreeing to talk to Bill, Jill took Andy into the house to clean up for supper. Alone, Reid limped his way down to one of the paddocks and, with the aide of one of the hands, saddled a horse. Kicking himself twelve ways from Sunday for having to put both Jill and Andy

LINDA CONRAD                    79

in the middle of an Operation Rock-A-Bye investigation, he rode out of the barn area and onto the open plain.

He was angry. Mad at the situation. Furious that he wanted her. Livid that he cared too much.

If he didn't know better, he'd be convinced he had a bad case of Austin's famous cedar fever, making him crazy.

Riding out across one of the Double B's pastures, Reid watched the sun glinting off one of the many coves long the shores of Long Lake in the distance. The last ten years dissolved as he was transported back to the impassioned days of his youth. That time, so many years ago, when he'd been so sure of himself, his goals and his darling Jill.

The two of them had spent hours riding in the hills around Rolling Point, planning their future. As soon as he'd passed the bar, he would've taken a job as assistant D.A. in Austin. Jill would've eventually gotten her law degree.

A few years of hard work later and they both would've joined his father-in-law's firm, right behind his best friend, Travis. The three of them would be the next bright generation of lawyers in the family.

His plan had been to eventually go into politics. He'd wanted to change the world for the better, with Jill by his side.

Hell. He'd been so naive. So gullible.

He spurred his mount to a gallop as the last ten years of his life dragged into his mind, reminding him of the pain and the heartache of growing up and finding out that all his solid foundations were mere figments of his imagination. Politicians couldn't change the world. There was a ruthless underbelly to life that would find a way around any law—or any man wanting to cure the evil.

The only way to make a dent in the darkness of crime was to be a lawman. Capture the criminals—the ones who broke the laws that politicians made. Put a finger in the dike of corruption. Slow the tide of evil in this world.

He also thought about how his own father had assumed the worst of him when he'd disappeared. His dad had always figured Reid for a no-good loser, because he hadn't wanted to be a rancher. When Reid disappeared on his wedding day, the man never gave another thought to his only son.

Jill's father, who Reid had always thought personified everything right on earth, also betrayed him on that last night for some reason. Reid was convinced it must've had to do with greed. His daughter, Jill, was just as bad, betraying him by hurrying into another marriage and having a child. She'd been spoiled, impressionable and weak.

At least, that was the way he'd always thought things had gone. Now he wasn't so sure.

Without thinking, he urged his horse to an all-out run when he began to contemplate about the way Jill had raised a son alone. And done a damn good job of it too. She'd gotten her law degree without Reid or her father's help and had continued with their old dream of changing the way things worked through politics.

Reid was impressed, though still stung by her past casual disregard. She hadn't come looking for him ten years ago. She'd pitched Reid's memory in the back seat of her mind and sped on with her life without him.

He wanted to hate her.

So many times during the last ten years he'd been sure he did hate her. Wanting to see her die a torturous death.

Reid came out of his daydream and found himself racing over the countryside with no consideration for his poor mount. He slowed the horse and pulled up under a stand of live oak. Both man and gelding were breathing hard.

He didn't hate Jill. Far from it. But his feelings for her were still a jumble. Every time he looked at her, tenderness, protectiveness and lust warred inside him.

No, he certainly didn't hate her.

So many things in his life were in a state of complete confusion. But his first loyalty had to be to Operation Rock-A-Bye. Find the bad guy. Finish the job.

Once that was done, he'd take a real leave of absence and spend the time here, investigating what his father-in-law had been involved with ten years ago. All his inquires back then had come to dead ends with Andrew's sudden death. But today he had training and contacts he never could have imagined possible.

Perhaps he'd also spend a little time figuring out how he really felt about Jill.

He'd already decided that he had to spend more time with her son. Andy was a too serious little boy who so obviously needed a father.

Reid dismounted and let his horse graze on the surrounding grass. Removing his satellite phone from its metal loop on his belt, he placed a call to a former special agent. A man who'd up until recently been part of his team.

As he listened to the phone ring he smiled, realizing he would be glad to hear the other man's voice. Reid needed someone with a clear head to help him evaluate the situation and the people involved. He knew he'd lost some of his objectivity here, and there was no one on the face of the planet whose good sense he trusted more than Deputy Manny Sanchez.

# Six

The next morning, Reid leaned his backside against a stucco column adjoining the ranch house patio, tipped his Stetson lower, and squinted through the blazing colors of the rising Texas sun. Pinks, deep blues and brilliant lavenders streamed around the early morning's patchy clouds, competing with the strains of softly bellowing cows and late crowing roosters for his attention.

He raised a steaming coffee mug to his lips and swallowed the black gold. Lord, it felt good to be back to his homeland. He'd never given Rolling Point a second thought when he decided not to return after being released from the hospital all those years ago.

Not that he hadn't thought plenty about some of the people here. All those months of lying there immobile and with his jaw wired shut, he'd dreamed of Jill. Of her, fighting to find him, torn and devastated with worry.

Ha! That was a joke. By the time his mother finally

located him with the help of a private detective, she told him that Jill had left for Paris and the rumor was that she'd married another man.

After he'd survived that blow to his ego, he built up enough walls to shield himself from the emotional pain. He figured he'd never return to this part of the country again.

Rachel, the kindhearted, physical therapist that Reid had hastily married before being released from the hospital, always swore he'd never be whole again until he faced his demons. For ten years he'd managed to dodge those perils.

If in all this time he hadn't really been whole, he'd sure done all right. Of course, he'd never felt the same kind of contentment anywhere else that he did standing here, looking out on this familiar countryside.

He should've tried coming home years ago.

Shaking his head at his own foolishness, he realized that his pride would never have let him confront Jill about her betrayal before now. To this day, he wondered if they would ever be able to discuss it openly.

A couple of times over the last weeks, Reid figured maybe they could have a relationship without ever delving into their past. Just build a new friendship and leave the old hurts buried. He wanted it badly. But since that spectacular kiss, he doubted if such a thing was possible.

Setting aside his coffee and wandering out past the white rails bordering the show ring, Reid's eye caught sight of a little paint in the working ring behind the foaling barn. She danced and pranced in the dusty, early morning, sunlight.

He rambled over and draped his arms over the fence to watch her cavorting.

"Mornin', Mr. Sorrels. Looks like that ankle of yourn's about healed up."

The Double B ranch hand, Bobby Ray, stepped to his side by the fence. Leaning against it, he lazily folded his arms across his chest, studying Reid while he watched the horse.

"Pretty little filly, ain't she?" Bobby Ray asked idly.

Reid nodded. "Why is she so full of life this morning?"

"I reckon it's cause that young Bennett boy's been working with her. He's the one who saddled her."

For the first time, Reid noticed the young paint was saddled and not looking the least bit happy about it.

"*Andy?* Where does he think he's going to ride her? She's too young to go very far."

In fact, the filly was too young and inexperienced for a child to ride—period.

Without waiting for an answer, Reid headed toward the barn behind the show ring. Approaching one of the stalls toward the rear of the barn, Reid was surprised to hear Andy softly talking. But he couldn't hear anyone else's voice. Was the kid talking to himself?

Quietly, he peered down over the stall door to find the boy standing with his back to the door, rope in hand and swinging it back and forth in front of a two- or three-month-old calf who cowered in the corner.

"Aw, come on, Essymae. Please stand still a minute. I won't hurt you. I just want to put this rope round your neck. I gotta practice, don't I?" Andy pleaded.

Reid knew Jill had forbidden the child to practice his roping or anything else without adult supervision. He also remembered distinctly explaining to Andy about the proper age and weight of the calves used for roping. This baby wasn't even weaned.

Judging by the early hour and the boy's secretive demeanor, the kid knew what he was up to would qualify as trouble—with a capital T.

"Mornin', son," Reid began, in his best "law officer" voice. "Do you have permission to be here today?"

Andy jerked around like he'd been stung. When he spotted Reid, he dropped the rope, jumped to attention and froze.

Reid didn't much care for the serious and frightened look on the child's face. He hadn't meant to scare him this badly. The poor kid was literally shaking in his boots.

Suddenly, Reid's protective reflexes kicked in. What Andy had done was misguided and childish, but not really bad enough for this much fear. Besides, the last thing he wanted was for the boy to be afraid of *him*.

Reid decided he'd better be cautious and careful of what he said and did next. He pushed his hat back off his forehead and softened his mouth into a grin.

"Just look at that poor baby. She's scared to death of you. I don't believe your mama raised you to be a bully, did she, boy?"

Andy fisted his hands and hesitatingly turned to the calf in the corner. Essymae provided a great sound effect at the exact right moment and issued a plaintive bleat. It did the trick.

Andy forgot about his own fear and went to the calf's side. "Oh, I'm so sorry, Essy. I didn't mean it." He knelt down and wrapped his arms around her neck. "I won't let anyone hurt you."

Reid watched the child with a soft swell of something that felt like pride. The boy had good instincts. Reid wasn't totally sure why that should make him proud, but he figured it had something to do with the fact that Jill was raising a basically good son, who would become a caring and fair man.

He'd been right about her all those years ago. She'd become a fantastic mother.

Reid bent on one knee beside Andy and put an arm around his shoulder. "You know you're not supposed to practice roping by yourself, don't you?"

The child lowered his head. "Yes, sir, but..." he said quietly.

"And you remember what I told you about how old a calf should be for roping?"

Andy nodded but didn't look up.

"Well, can you tell me what you were thinking?"

A pair of ebony-colored eyes hazarded a glance at him. Reid could see the fight between wanting to do the right thing and wanting to do the fun thing going on behind those eyes. His heart went out to the boy.

"I was wr-wrong, sir. I should be punished," Andy admitted.

Reid felt a clutch around his heart. Watching this child own up to his wrongdoing and be sincerely sorry was giving Reid a sympathetic ache. He wanted to wrap his arms around him and protect the boy from all the bad things that would happen in the rest of his life. But he knew that Andy would never allow anyone to baby him.

"Knowing you've made a mistake is the first step to being a man." Reid watched the guilt begin to turn into hope. "If you were the grown-up here, what punishment would be appropriate?"

"I..."

Reid knew how hard that question would be for a child to answer. It wouldn't be a snap for an adult. He held his breath and waited.

"I shouldn't be allowed to go to the rodeo this weekend, sir.'' The bleak look in Andy's eyes clearly told Reid exactly how difficult that answer had been.

Reid nearly broke down and hugged him. He truly was a remarkable child.

''Hmm. And what do you think your mother will say when she finds out?''

Andy straightened and, this time, the serious look was not frightened but remorseful. ''She'll be hurt that I disobeyed.''

''Hurt, but not mad? She won't yell and send you to your room?''

''Oh no. She never yells. She loves me.'' The beginnings of a tear formed in the corner of Andy's eye for the first time since being caught.

At this moment, Reid knew he would always love this sensitive child, too. ''Maybe we'd be better off not telling her?''

''No, sir,'' the boy said softly. ''That wouldn't be the honest thing to do.''

Reid heard a soft groan behind him. He'd thought he'd felt someone's presence nearby earlier, but he'd been so wrapped up in Andy he ignored it.

He stood and moved to the side so both he and Andy could face the intruder. It was Jill. Reid wondered how long she'd been standing there and how much she'd heard.

''There you two are.'' She breezed into the stall and smiled. ''I wondered where you'd gotten off to at such an early hour. Aren't you ready for breakfast yet?''

Reid took in everything about her in an instant. He missed nothing. Not the crystal-blue eyes about to brim over with tears. Not the pencil-slim jeans, hugging her rounded hips. Nor the rise and fall of her cropped top under the hand she'd placed against her breast.

The cornflower-blue top she wore was the same color as her eyes, but it couldn't compete with the milky white-ness of the skin showing both above and below it. And nothing could compete with her soft and compelling gaze. It was hesitant, but anxious. Concerned, but loving.

All of a sudden, Reid's heart went out to the mother as well as the son. He wanted desperately to help her. But he had no business butting in. He didn't really belong here.

Andy finally broke the silence. "I did a bad thing, Mom."

The boy eased his hand into Reid's and squeezed, ask-ing for strength through his touch. "I came out here to practice my roping alone. I'm sorry."

Jill rushed to her son's side, but slowed before she got there and knelt in the dust in front of him. "Can we talk about this for a minute?"

Andy nodded, watching her carefully.

"What exactly are you sorry for?"

"I'm...I'm sorry I disobeyed you." A gleam in his eyes told her that's what he figured she wanted to hear.

"I see. Well, that's a good thing. Are you sorry about anything else?"

Andy considered that for minute. Finally, his head came up and he looked at Reid. "I'm sorry I didn't listen to Reid and did everything wrong. I'm sorry I'm going to be punished." He took a breath and blurted out his final apology. "And I'm really, really sorry I scared Essymae. I'll never do it again. I promise."

Reid studied Jill's face. She had a couple of hard de-cisions to make here. Ones that might affect her child and their relationship forever. Again he wished he could do something to ease her way.

She reached out and gingerly touched her baby's

cheek. Reid figured she'd fold Andy into her embrace and soothe away his emotional turmoil. That's sure what he'd been wanting to do since he'd first found the boy here.

Instead, Jill brought her hand back to her side and stood. "Have you really learned something?" she probed.

"Yes, ma'am." The guilt was back in Andy's whole demeanor. He looked scared and defeated and he sniffed back a sob.

"A good man takes care of all the people and things that are weaker than he is. He never takes advantage of them. I love you, son, with my whole heart. I want you to grow up to be a good and caring man." The tip of her tongue slipped out of the corner of her mouth as she considered her options.

"I'm proud of you for being honest," she finally said. "Can you tell me what you're going to do about this?"

Andy slowly nodded his head. "Next time I'm going to think real hard about who's going to be hurt if I do something."

The corners of Jill's mouth creased into a near smile, but she held off. "That's good." She bent her head and lowered her voice. "And what should *I* do about this now, Andy?"

"You should punish me, Mom." His shoulders began to sag as he added, "I shouldn't be allowed to go to the rodeo this weekend."

Jill sighed deeply. "I'm not sure yet if we're even going to rodeo this weekend. But if that's a possibility, not letting you go would be as much of a punishment for Reid and me as it would be for you."

Andy couldn't stand still. He ran to his mother and threw his arms around her waist.

"I'm so sorry I hurt you, Mom," he sobbed.

Reid's knees were weak with wanting to go to them both. Wanting to soothe and somehow make things right. But he stood rooted and watched.

Jill put her arms around Andy and hugged him to her. "I know you are. I love you all the more for it."

She eased him back and put her hand under his chin, raising his face so he could see her eyes. "You're a good person, son." She put her other hand over his heart. "In here, where it counts the most."

Jill took one step back and straightened her shoulders. "I think the best thing for you to do is to take some time and really listen to what's in your heart. You need to think through what you've learned."

Andy mimicked her stance and prepared himself for the worst.

"For the rest of the week, you will not ride or practice your roping. Instead, you'll spend the time currying the horses, bringing feed to the pens and mucking out stalls." She grinned down at the top of his head. "Learn what the animals need. Listen to them. Befriend them. If you want to use them for fun, you should be able to see it from their point of view as well as your own."

The boy's eyes grew wide and he nodded quickly.

"If it's possible for us to go to both the regatta and the rodeo, we'll all go together. It won't hurt you to see that real cowboys respect their animals and treat them with kindness if you're going to be there someday."

Relief and happiness spread across Andy's features. He hugged Jill again. "I love you, Mom."

Reid came to a rather startling conclusion right then. He loved her too. He'd never stopped loving her. With every fiber of his being and every beat of his heart.

He knew she loved him too. She didn't really care for

that Baldwin guy. Reid had known it by the way she'd kissed him at the hospital. Known it also by the way she looked at him and lowered her voice when she spoke. He just hadn't opened his heart and soul up to listen to hers.

No more. Reid wasn't afraid of being hurt anymore. The pain and the doubting were behind them. He suddenly knew the past meant nothing. It could stay buried for all he cared. The future was all that mattered. His future with Jill and her son.

He would find a way to be with her and her good-hearted child forever. No more what-ifs and should'ves. The girl he'd loved so long ago was gone, but the woman she'd been inside was what had drawn him then, and that was what would keep him by her side throughout eternity now.

They belonged together. Irrevocably joined by their love.

He would make sure that happened. He was no longer the boy he'd been back then, either. Today he was a man of conviction and determination—not easily dissuaded or discouraged. Nothing would stop him from convincing her that they belonged together. Not a job, not a fiancé—nothing and no one.

When Jill stepped into her mother's kitchen, the smell of sizzling bacon and steaming coffee nearly knocked her over, reminding her that none of them had eaten yet. She sent Andy to wash up and change his shirt while she told the cook what they'd like for breakfast.

Reid poured them both mugs of dark, rich coffee, set them down on the huge kitchen table, then went to wash up himself.

The ambiance in the ranch's gigantic kitchen seemed cozy and warm. Even though it was the middle of June,

the early mornings in the hill country still carried a bit
of a chill. But here, in her mother's idea of an industrial
but homespun kitchen, a fire had been laid in the hearth,
gleaming brass-bottom pans hung from above the cook-
top and two dozen tiny pots full of herbs sat in the green-
house window still glistening from their morning misting.

Sitting down at the rough-sawn, wooden table that
could seat twelve, Jill blew on the hot liquid in one of
the mugs and tried to sort through the swirling impulses
assailing her.

Had she done the best she could with her son this
morning? She didn't know for sure what the best thing
was. Andy was her first experience at being a parent and
she had no one to talk to about it. Many times in the past
she'd wished that Andy had a father, not only for his
sake, but for her own peace of mind as well.

A man's opinion would've been invaluable. After all,
what did she really know about being a man?

The fact that Andy's real father had been only a few
feet away during their conversation this morning made
taking the whole responsibility alone that much more difficult. She'd overheard the concern and caring in Reid's
voice when he'd spoken to Andy. It was lucky for her
that Andy's need had been so great and so immediate.
Otherwise, she might have broken down and told them
both the truth on the spot.

And that would not have been a very intelligent thing
to do. They both deserved to know, but she needed to
find a way to break it to them gently. She knew that
simply blurting it out could cause no end of problems—
for them as well as for her.

Her thoughts shifted to the one main reason she wanted
desperately to tell the truth. Reid. She was beginning to
ease back into old her familiar feelings about the man.

The exquisitely sensual longing. The building, pulsating craving that seemed to slowly occupy more and more of her mind.

For a long time, it had been as if a piece was missing from the jigsaw puzzle of her life—the king of hearts lost from her deck. Silly, but when Reid was nearby, she knew all the missing pieces had been found. Perhaps still not in proper order or perspective, but close at hand.

Jill took a swallow of coffee, burnt her tongue and once again blew lightly on the steaming liquid. She found herself arguing both sides of the dilemma. She and Reid had too many problems to ever go back to where they'd been.

He was still the sexiest man alive, and even today he could make her feel like he could right any wrong or capture any star from the sky. But she was afraid that she'd never really be able to forgive the callous way he'd used her. When she thought back to how hurt and embarrassed she'd been when he'd left her before their wedding, she knew she'd never fully trust him with her heart again.

To make matters infinitely worse, her guilt about not finding a way to tell him about his son long before now was building to unbearable proportions. Her pride might be standing in their way now, but his anger over not getting to know his son would be an irrevocable source of division.

The trouble was, she'd sell her soul to have one more hour in his arms, one more night to forget herself in the roaring rampage of his kisses.

What would their relationship be as they both worked together to raise their son? She was positive now that he would want to play a role in Andy's upbringing. He had

that right. But what part, if any, would she and Reid play
in each other's lives?

All of those things raced through her mind, then lodged
in her throat when Reid sauntered through the doorway.
He'd changed into a saddle-colored, muscle enhancing
T-shirt and had raked his fingers through his wet hair in
an effort to remove the hat marks. She blew out a breath
and blinked. The man simply reeked of potent masculin-
ity.

From across the room, his dark, compelling eyes lingered on her like a red-hot caress. Turning, he retrieved
two plates of food from the cook at the other end of the
kitchen and set one down in front of her and one at another place.

"Did I guess right on which one is yours and which
is Andy's?" he asked, pulling out a chair at a third place
and straddling it.

"Yes, thank you." His simple gesture caused a flut-
tering sensation in her stomach that had nothing whatever
to do with food. "Aren't you going to eat, too?"

He picked up his mug and took a gulp of the black
brew. "Not this morning, thanks." He took a second sip
and moaned his appreciation. "Mmm. I'm sure going to
miss the great coffee around here. Nobody makes it quite
this way."

"Mother uses a variety of imported beans and..." The
truth hit her squarely between the eyes. "You're leaving
soon?"

His heavy-lidded gaze stayed locked with hers. "Will
you miss me when I'm gone?"

The smirk of masculine ego in his expression strength-
ened the delicious throbbing between her legs she'd
failed to notice before. She squeezed her knees together

in order to stem the insistent pulsing and cleared her throat to cover her hoarse voice.

"Where are you going? Is your ankle that much better?" she rasped.

"It's time I went back to Mom's, Jill. I really appreciate your hospitality, but the ankle's good enough for me to drive, and I have some things I should be doing."

By the time she'd recovered her voice, he'd gotten up, swung his chair around and downed the last of his coffee.

"You sure you'll be all right?" she murmured.

"No sweat. I'll be fine." He sat the mug on the counter and then stood, towering over her. "I wanted to tell you what a great job I thought you did with Andy this morning. You were spectacular."

Depthless, dark eyes hinted at the undercurrents of something vibrant and cosmic between them. He reached out and gently tucked one of her wayward curls behind an ear.

Letting his fingers linger on her earlobe for the longest time, he finally sighed, then spoke. "You're a terrific mother, sweetheart."

Jill stopped breathing and closed her eyes. Need, guilt and just plain old lust battled inside her.

"I recall a night long ago when I told you that you'd make the best mother ever. Remember?"

How could she ever forget that night? The sound of their favorite music suddenly filled her ears, and the tingling remnants of remembered passion leaped through her blood.

Forget that night? Impossible.

The memory of the erotic and narcotic friction of his steeled muscles against her yielding flesh, her crisp sheets sliding under their steamy bodies, the heady taste of champagne on his tongue as he kissed her lips—all came back in a flash, giving her flushed warmth and shivers of longing.

Forget the night that Andy was conceived? Never.

"We were rather young and impetuous back then, Reid. If we'd only known..."

"Known what the future would bring? That's never possible, Jill. All we can do is live in the now and take each new dawn as it comes. The past is over. The future may never be."

The connection Jill felt to him at that moment was so acute that she believed every word he hadn't spoken.

Everything would work out—somehow.

"Will you call me when you know for sure about Saturday?" he asked.

She nodded, wondering how to get to see him before then. She wanted him. Wanted him back in her bed. She could swear that he wanted her, too.

Their day of reckoning was still in a future that might never be. Meanwhile, one more taste of the paradise of his kiss couldn't be wrong. They'd just shared intimate memories. Surely they could share one more moment of magic.

"But... But I thought we were going to talk. We haven't had a chance. And what about Andy?"

He moved toward the door, turning back to search her eyes. "I need to see a friend this morning, and I might be a little busy for a few days. But if you... or Andy...needs anything, just call."

He walked out the door, leaving her sitting at the table alone. She tried to get herself under control. Had she gone nuts for a moment?

She had no business wanting him. There couldn't be any magic moments in their future. When he learned the

truth, an unbridgeable distance would probably come between them. If she seduced him before that, he'd likely
never speak to her again. And what would that mean
for Andy?

# Seven

**R**eid flexed his ankle and pressed down on the accelerator. Damn, but it felt good to be back behind the wheel of a truck.

While on the Double B, he'd been glad for the opportunity to ride something besides a desk or an FBI issued vehicle.

But horses could only take you so far. To meet Manny Sanchez in San Antonio, he needed motorized transportation.

Watching the dusty miles tick by, Reid enjoyed the freedom of independence, the feeling of being master of his own fate once more. He knew the exhilaration wouldn't last. After all, he was back to the investigation in earnest. But as he drove toward the city, he let the warm feelings he'd had all morning wash over him again.

It had been nearly impossible for him to walk away from Jill at the kitchen table. But it was the proper thing to do. The timing wasn't right for them yet. First, he needed answers to his questions about Baldwin.

Reid hoped to find reasons enough for Jill to be free to accept that she still loved him. Just putting Baldwin on the suspect list was one thing, proving he'd had anything to do with the baby-selling scheme was entirely another.

Reid had seen the way Jill's eyes glazed over at the table this morning. They'd both been surrounded by sweet memories of shared passions. She'd been so sensitive to his desires.

They'd always been so hot together. He'd suspected that she'd never forgotten that. He knew he certainly hadn't.

In that moment, when she'd closed her eyes for a second, Reid guessed she'd been trembling with need. Lost in the desire that raged between them to this day.

He'd fed the flames, almost without thinking it through. He'd wanted her to need him again, with the same intensity as he needed her. But it was just a little too soon to complete this reawakening.

First he must find the proof that would implicate Baldwin and get him out of her life. He knew it must be there. All he had to do was turn over the right rock.

Jill crossed her legs under the cloth-covered table and took a sip of wine. Having lunch with Bill in this fancy restaurant near the capital was not the way she'd have chosen to spend her time today. But there were a few things that needed to be settled.

"I'm sorry I was going out of town the other night when you called me," Bill began. "Is Andy all right?"

"Yes, he's fine. But, uh…" Jill set her glass down and firmed her resolve to say what had to be said. "I must tell you something, Bill. Coming so close to losing him has made me reexamine my life.''

Bill narrowed his eyes and took a sip from his own glass. ''And what conclusions have you reached?''

She took a deep breath and rushed ahead. ''I'm sorry, but the truth is, I don't love you. Not the way a wife should feel about her husband.''

He visibly relaxed his shoulders and smiled at her. ''Don't worry about that. You'll learn. Most great marriages are built on mutual respect and trust. It takes time to grow into a loving relationship. My parents never loved one another, but they had a long and fruitful marriage.''

''That's not the way I want to live. I've decided that I'd rather live alone for the rest of my life than to marry someone I don't really love.'' She held out her hand, palm up, in a pleading gesture. ''Please understand.''

Bill's cheeks flushed and his jaw ticked as he studied her with an intense perusal. ''Is there someone else?''

''No. Not...really.'' She jerked her hand back and placed both hands in her lap. ''This is a decision I've been considering for quite a while. I believe it will be in everybody's best interest. I'm truly sorry.''

He didn't miss a beat. ''Will you still be my campaign manager?''

Jill was a little taken aback by how quickly he'd recovered his composure. ''Of course I will. I wouldn't leave you stranded at the last minute.''

''And you'll still be a hostess for the Lake Austin regatta this Saturday?'' he demanded.

''Uh. I wanted to talk to you about that, too.''

''You can't renege on this, Jill. Your cousin Travis already backed out on me this morning. He'd promised to carry the governor on his yacht in the parade of sails.

Now Travis says we can use his schooner but he's too busy to be there himself. You'll have to take over as skipper and sail his yacht in the parade.''

"What? But I don't know how to sail. I can't be a skipper.''

"You must know how. You grew up around here. Everyone knows how to sail.''

"Well, I don't.''

"Then you'd better learn in a hurry.'' Bill set down his wineglass and motioned to the waiter that he was prepared to order.

He lifted his chin, turning back to her. "This is one of the most important events we've scheduled for our pre-campaign activities. You were the main organizer, re-member?

"It's the least you can do after backing out of our engagement. I refuse to be further embarrassed by having to move the governor and his wife when they already expect to be on Travis's boat.'' The waiter arrived and Bill picked up his menu. "Learn to sail or find someone else to do it. Either way, you and the governor's party will be aboard that boat on Saturday. It's your responsi-bility.''

A couple of hours after leaving Rolling Point, Reid pulled the truck into the parking lot of the FBI's regional office in San Antonio, and checked his watch. A few minutes early. Manny wouldn't have been able to drive here from his new home in Willow Springs in such a short time.

Until last fall, Manny Sanchez had been Reid's right-hand man in the field. They'd worked on Operation Rock-A-Bye together for over six years. Then last De-cember, as they were wrapping up a sting near Del Rio,

Manny had fallen hard for a young woman he'd been forced to use as part of the assignment.

The lure of love, family, and the home life Manny had never known proved to be stronger than anything the FBI had to offer. Reid was secretly glad his friend found what he'd always seemed to have needed.

Manny left the Bureau and had taken a job as the local deputy sheriff. But not before he'd captured one of the midlevel cogs they'd been seeking in the international crime syndicate—that gang of creeps, specializing in stealing babies from all over the world and selling them to rich U.S. couples desperate enough to pay outrageous sums. The man Manny arrested had pointed them to Austin and directly to the state lawmakers.

Reid parked and, after passing through security, found the cafeteria. He'd promised to meet Manny there, before the two of them entered the secured conference room Reid had ordered for their think tank session.

Twenty minutes and another cup of coffee later, Reid spied Manny as he appeared in the doorway to the cafeteria. He looked good. Dressed casually in jeans and long-sleeved shirt, he seemed a few pounds heavier than the last time Reid had seen him, but on Manny the added weight appeared healthy. His hair was considerably shorter than the last time, too. He looked exactly like a happily married man who worked in public law enforcement—and loved it.

A prick of jealousy pierced Reid's inner shell, but he stuffed the emotion back into the corners of his heart where it belonged. He was truly happy for Manny, and he was very glad that his old friend had agreed to spend a couple of days advising Reid on his current suspect.

"*Qué paso,* boss," Manny said as he swung past Reid's table and headed for the coffeepot.

When he'd poured himself a cup, he returned to sit across from Reid. "How's the investigation going?"

"I'm not your boss, Sanchez. You know the name's Reid...and the investigation stinks." He took a final swallow of coffee. "Thanks for coming. I figure it must be tough to leave your family."

Right after they'd married six months ago, Manny and his new wife adopted a baby that had been directly involved in their meeting. Reid helped with the paperwork.

Manny's eyes glinted in the fluorescent light. "Tougher than you know. Randi just told me last night that our family is about to grow."

"A child? You and Randi are expecting?" That same stab of jealousy came back to bite Reid in the heart.

He shook off the alien weakness and related what he'd found in Austin so far. Manny still had full security clearance, and Reid's former underling could think circles around the department's criminal analysts. His years in the field meant he could get into the head of the bad guys and ferret out what their next moves might be.

Reid wanted the two of them to find the key that would narrow the field of suspects down to Baldwin. It was the best way he knew to get the man out of his path to Jill. He hoped if he gave Manny enough information, they'd figure out a plan of action together.

After a cursory explanation, the two agents moved into a specially designed conference room. Reid had ordered computers, satellite phones, decent chairs and a sofa. Printouts of all the previous six years' worth of investigations for Operation Rock-A-Bye lay scattered across the broad slick surface of one of the mahogany conference tables.

Reid also had obtained all the necessary approvals to use the Bureau's computer research files and secured Internet access. With the option of ordering food in and a refrigerator already stocked with drinks, Reid prepared to hunker down for as long as it took to get his answers.

Their move to the conference room gave Manny time to think over the facts as Reid related them. "Okay. Let's say for the moment, the Bureau's intelligence was flawed and Baldwin should have been put on the list of possible suspects," Manny began as he settled down. "What do we know about his background?"

Reid handed him the dossier they'd gathered on the Texas attorney general. "This is only a partially complete file. Intelligence didn't have much time to compile all the facts."

"Hmm." Manny noted the file number on the folder in his hand and turned around to punch a few strokes into the computer behind him. "Are they still adding info?"

"As we speak."

A couple of minutes later, Manny rested his hands on the keyboard. "There's a few glaring holes in this file so far. Go away for an couple hours and give me some time to do a little research on my own."

"You going to go through regular channels? Won't that take forever? Just give Intelligence a little more time."

Manny grinned at his old boss, rolling his eyes in mock exasperation. "Takes too long. I have my own channels, thanks." He looked back at the blinking screen and began to type. "Go away," he muttered over his shoulder.

Reid spent the time checking with his INS and border patrol contacts. He wanted to know if there were any new rumors about baby-selling activity around the Texas border. Since Operation Rock-A-Bye pulled in that last middleman, the crime syndicate boss had either backed down on his activities or he'd buried the illegal operation so far underground that the FBI would never be able to dig them out. Reid fervently prayed they'd forced their man to the edge.

In exactly two hours, Reid was back in the conference room and seated next to Manny and his computer. "Well?"

"Odds are, Baldwin is not our man," Manny said quietly but with assurance.

"What? How can you be so sure?"

"Do you have some old grudge against this guy from your college days?"

"No, of course not."

Manny shrugged. "Then I can't imagine why you'd consider jumping him onto the suspect list. He doesn't fit the profile at all." Manny narrowed his eyes to study Reid. "And I know you'd have already figured that out if there wasn't some kind of trouble between you two."

Reid swallowed hard and fought the urge to argue with his friend. But he trusted Manny's judgment implicitly.

"Maybe I've been a little hasty. Convince me I'm wrong," he urged.

Manny turned back to the blinking screen and pointed to a list of numbers. "For one thing, not enough money."

"Huh?"

"You know as well as I do that there are big bucks in baby-selling. *Mega* bucks. One kid with the right coloring can bring in as much as a quarter of a million dollars."

He tapped a finger on the keyboard and another list appeared. "But Baldwin's finances don't add up to anything like that. To run for governor, he's had to file disclosure statements with the state's elections board. His campaign committee does have millions, but they can account for every penny."

Manny smiled at the screen and continued. "I also

have a buddy who works as an investigative reporter for the Fort Worth *Star-Telegram*. He's been digging for years into Baldwin's financial dealings, trying to find the dirt. But there are no hidden bank accounts. No phony corporations to launder the money. No nothing. The guy's clean.''

Reid sank into his chair. He couldn't believe he'd stepped out of character so far as to allow himself to be blindsided by his desire for Jill. He needed to get back on track.

''What else?'' he probed.

''The man we're looking for must have contacts and private offices to work from. But he doesn't necessarily have to have connections to any government officials in Mexico.'' Manny clicked a couple of keys and the screen blinked on a new page. ''In this millennium, all you need is a computer hacker or two on your payroll. They break into any government system they want, alter a few records, and poof, they have whatever documents they need.''

''Like what kind of documents?''

''Birth certificates. Immigration records. Marriage certificates. You name it.''

Reid gave the computer a suspicious glance. ''Does that help us narrow it down to who's in charge?''

Manny turned to him. ''Maybe. All we need to do is track down the hackers.''

''Is that all?'' Reid grumbled. ''That could take months.''

''You've been buried in your own mission too long, old buddy. The Bureau has ten different operations going right now that involve the use of the cyber-technology section. The nation's security depends on the integrity of the Internet and our government's computerized systems.''

''And?''

''Let me contact an old friend or two in the Bureau,'' Manny added. ''Maybe we can get a quick approval from the Justice Department for the use of one of their track and trace devices for a few days. We'll be able to backtrack our man through the system. We'll hack into *his* operation and have him cold.''

Reid needed to move. Needed to begin hunting for the right man. Needed to find the right way to get back to Jill.

''Can you handle this alone?'' he asked.

''No problem. Let me take one of the Bureau's satellite computers with me, and I can run the whole thing from home.''

''Do it,'' Reid urged fiercely. ''Oh, and Manny...'' As he picked up a portable phone to issue the orders, Reid stopped for a second, the phone suspended in midair. ''Thanks for making me face reality. You saved my hide. I owe you.''

The day after her lunch with Bill, Jill took the afternoon off. She squinted up into the glare of the noonday sun and pulled a pair of sunglasses out of her floppy bag. It had been years since she'd even placed a big toe in Long Lake. Slipping on her shorts this morning, she'd been dismayed at how pale her skin looked.

The lake hadn't changed much, she thought as she stepped out onto the quiet dock. Since the property surrounding the lake was mostly owned by ranchers in the area, very little development marred the landscape. This marina with its tiny gas dock, even smaller café, and a few scattered homes on the hillsides were the only signs of civilization.

As teens, she and her friends had literally lived on the lake every summer. They'd taken motorboat rides, water-skied, even did personal watercraft racing—before the county outlawed it.

Most of the year, kids in the area had ranch chores to do before school, riding lessons to take or give and, over all, just be busy young Texans. But during the summer months, everyone found some time to spend on or in the water.

In college, the main weekend activity had been tubing down one of the rivers near Austin, with beer kegs tied to one of the inner tubes, floating beside them. But in high school, it had been the many lake activities that held the young people's attention.

All that was long ago and far away from the person she was today. Mother, attorney, campaign manager.

"Jill," Reid called to her, breaking into her thoughts as he walked toward the dock where she stood. "What's this all about?"

The man looked positively wicked today in his khaki shorts and a pale yellow T-shirt, loosely covering his broad chest. Her heart thumped wildly in her own chest and she fought her lustful impulses so she could tell him why she'd called for help.

"You said you knew how to sail. That you can skipper any boat with a mast. Well, I need to learn how."

"Now? Today?" He stepped onto the dock and grinned. "Can't this wait for a better time?"

She shook her head. "I wish it could wait forever. But I guess I have no choice."

He picked up the cooler she'd set down by her feet and studied her face. "I vaguely remember that you were

never very interested in sailing. You always said you
wanted the security of a motor-powered craft…that you
didn't like being at the mercy of the wind. What's happened?''

"It's a long story. But it's imperative I learn how.''
She waved her hand toward the small sloop she'd bor-
rowed, indicating that they should climb aboard while she
still had the nerve. "This is a girlfriend's boat. She said
we could borrow it for a few hours. Do you think it'll
take that long to teach me to sail?''

He chuckled and swung himself and the cooler onto
the deck. "Things take however long they take. Learning
to sail in one afternoon seems like pushing it, though.''

He set the cooler down and reached a suntanned arm
up to give her a steadying hand. "Will you explain why
it's so important to rush this?''

"Later.'' She placed a soft-soled, canvas shoe onto the
edge of the gently shifting boat and jumped, landing with
a thunk against Reid's body and nearly knocking him
down.

He threw his arms around her in an instinctual move
to keep them both upright. The gut level reaction she'd
had when jammed against his muscled chest annoyed her.
She simply didn't have time today for her body to be
aroused by an accident of proximity.

She pulled back, intending to move away from him
and the temptation he represented. Reid tightened his grip
on her and searched her eyes behind the sunglasses for
the connection he knew they both had felt.

The blazing sun heated her skin while the sultry gaze
he gave her heated places you couldn't see. He'd aroused
her with merely a touch, a glance, a muffled groan.

*Not now, please.* She begged her body to behave.
There wasn't time. This wasn't the place.

"What'll I do first?" Gathering her wits and her determination, she shoved gently at his waist and he let go.

Reid quickly stowed the cooler inside the little cabin and came back toward her, donning a baseball cap he'd found there. "Do you remember back to our motorboat days when I taught you how to cast off?"

"Sort of." Mostly what she remembered from that time was being young and in love. The memories became stronger with every ragged breath.

"Just hang on to the dock for a second," he scoffed.

She did as he asked and within a few minutes they were drifting away from land. Reid checked the wind direction and frowned up at the gathering dark clouds on the horizon.

Usually, the winds were brisk on Long Lake. But with a storm threatening to move in later tonight, the breeze had died and the sticky, stale air barely stirred. The water softly lapped against the sides of the sloop.

"We've got a small problem," he admitted. "It's going to take two of us to get out of this tight harbor with so little wind. And you won't be much help, I'm afraid."

She grinned up at him. "I can follow instructions perfectly well. Show me what you want me to do."

# Eight

"**Y**ou man the tiller," Reid grumbled. "I'll raise the mainsail."

When Jill mentioned being capable of following instructions, from somewhere out of the misty past, he remembered everything he'd ever taught her. He'd fought off the bombarding images of her naked, rising over him with the same seductive smile on her face that she now wore. His mind refused to let go of their hot, sensual lessons.

Reid needed to get a grip. He wasn't a horny young kid anymore. Adult enough to put his pulsating desires on hold, he vowed to wait, at least, until he found a way to make sure she didn't love Baldwin.

"What's the tiller?" she asked, turning toward the sloop's stern in the direction he'd indicated.

He showed her where to sit and lightly placed her hands on the smooth, wooden bar. "As I recall, you used to be fairly proficient at driving a ski-boat. The tiller is the steering wheel. It's attached to the rudder.''

She let her palms slide lazily up and down the long, glossy handle.

In those thigh-topping white shorts and white eyelet, short-sleeved blouse that tied at the waist, she was exactly the picture of perfection he remembered. She'd pulled back her thick mane of ebony curls into a loose ponytail, making those blue-ice eyes stand out starkly against the creamy background of her cheeks. That is, they did when she took off the sunglasses long enough to see them.

The woman was very nearly too beautiful to bear.

He hissed out a pent-up breath and stepped away from her, determined to continue the cursory instructions from a distance. "Just remember that when I tell you to go left, you push the tiller to the right—and vice versa.''

Reid unfisted his hands long enough to take off his shoes and moved up the starboard passenger seat to the bulkhead and rigging. As he unfurled the sails and put the boom behind him, he caught a glimpse of Jill as she screwed up her mouth and worked at keeping the bow where she thought it should go while they glided gingerly away from the marina.

With little makeup and those impossible Hollywood sunglasses, she looked fifteen again. The same fresh-faced dynamo he'd wooed and won. He noticed her tongue peeking out between her lips while she was lost in concentration and his heart was totally lost in return.

Keeping both the jib sheet and the mainsheet in his hand, he moved back to sit across from her. "You doing okay?"

She nodded but didn't take her eyes off the horizon.

He gave her a couple of general sailing instructions and watched her smile as the sloop responded to her touch.

The muggy weather and still back bay began to take its toll on them both. While he gazed at her, sweat broke out on her forehead, trickled down her cheeks and long slender neck. At last, it dripped shamelessly to her breasts and slowly disappeared into the valley between. With such a sight, his own overheated skin broke into a million tiny jets of itchy, tingling sweat that he tried his damnedest to ignore.

"Sure hope the wind picks up when we hit open water," he gurgled past the sudden lump in his throat. "Otherwise, this might turn into a very short and sweltering lesson."

"I'm sure the wind will cooperate." She hazarded a glance in his direction. "And maybe the rain will show up early to cool us off."

"Maybe." He studied her profile and eased off the sails, giving them plenty of leeway. "But if that storm closes in before dark, it'll be an old-fashioned gully washer."

"Mmm." Another smile bubbled across her face.

"You worried, or hopeful?" he asked casually.

"Hopeful." She beamed at him and pushed gently on the tiller. "It's been years since I've been outdoors in a rainstorm without running for cover. When I was little, I remember loving the cool feel of the rain on my skin on a hot day and of all the fun Travis and I used to have trying to catch raindrops with our tongues."

It was Reid's turn to smile at the thought of her as a mischievous pixie dancing through the rain. He leaned back and watched the bald cypress and stately pecan trees pass by on the shore as the sloop slowly made its way out of the harbor. He took a deep breath and thought he smelled the pungent odor of ozone that permeates the air right before the rain begins.

But then, maybe he just wished for it to be so for Jill's sake.

When they reached the open water of Long Lake's main bay, Jill relaxed enough to kick off her deck shoes and put her feet up on the shelf where he sat. Putting one foot on either side of his hips, she leaned back and raised her chin to the sun.

"I'd forgotten how much I love it out here," she said with a sigh.

He wanted her to remember how she'd loved other things as well. But he had a big problem to dispense with first. They needed to have a long discussion.

"Jill, tell me what was so important that you had to take a day off to learn to sail?" He wanted to get her talking.

"I had lunch with Bill yesterday."

Reid caught the frown, pinching the bridge of her nose before she continued. "I wanted to ask him about you going along to the regatta so you could take us to the rodeo afterward, but I didn't get the chance. He informed me that I had to skipper Travis's sailboat in the sail parade on Saturday." She sighed. "I guess my cousin found something he'd rather do than play host to the governor."

"And you are forced to do as Bill demands because...?"

She slanted a dark look at Reid, but quickly looked back to the bow.

"I was the one who thought up this fund-raiser months ago. I've done everything I could think of to publicize it and Bill's campaign. The governor holds the big key to

Bill's getting the party's nomination. I don't want anything to jeopardize that or to make the governor angry.''

Reid's mission for Operation Rock-A-Bye meant he needed to go to that fund-raiser. But he decided all this talk about Baldwin was a good opportunity to get a couple of things out in the sunshine first.

"Sweetheart, why haven't you been wearing Bill's ring lately? Is there something wrong between you two?"

Jill bit down on her lip and threw a quick, furtive glance in his direction before answering. "I know it looked like I accepted his proposal the night of the ballroom fund-raiser, but I never did." She took a deep breath. "For your information, I wouldn't go around kissing other men if I were truly engaged."

She threw him a pointed look and pushed the sunglasses higher on the bridge of her nose. "I insisted he take back the ring that same night. Yesterday I told him to stop hoping...that we'll never be married."

"Did you decide you didn't want the loss of privacy that being married to the next governor would mean?" he asked warily.

"Nope. I decided I didn't want to be married to someone I don't love. I've never really loved Bill, and now I know that I never could."

Reid stifled a sigh. His shoulders felt lighter, and the whole day seemed brighter somehow.

Almost as soon as that thought came, another stronger sensation hit him. Where the heat of the afternoon had been sticky and uncomfortable before, his body now felt on fire. Unbearable needles of electricity burned through his veins.

The lonely, gray desolation that had been his life for so long, cleared away enough for him to see the patchy turquoise skies beyond.

But the time still wasn't right for them. Jill might not want Baldwin, but she also hadn't made it clear she wanted Reid. He couldn't look at her, so he glanced down at his hands and found them shaking uncontrollably.

Any other discussions they needed to have, would have to wait. He couldn't manage to be coherent now if his life depended on it.

"I think I'd better check the…uh…water depth," he sputtered. "There's a couple of shallow spots out here. I don't want us to get into trouble." He stood, swung himself over her outstretched legs and moved to the bow in record time.

Jill watched him stand on the bow with his back to her, checking the sails and gazing out over the clear, blue water. Just how the heck was she supposed to concentrate on sailing when her view of the horizon was blocked by the most amazing specimen of manhood she could ever remember seeing?

The yellow T-shirt he wore, that earlier fit him loosely and now was soaked with sweat, clung to his sculpted contours. That spectacular vision forced a curling warmth to race along her arteries, moving to her center core. She tried harder to think about the direction the boat was headed, but found herself, instead, considering what the muscles of his chest would look like with no shirt at all.

This was definitely not the same male body she'd known so well as a girl.

That thought made her become ever more aware she didn't really know this new Reid. He didn't look quite the same, his voice was deeper now, and he'd apparently given up his old dreams of getting justice and right through the law and politics. Who was he now?

Yesterday at the breakfast table, she'd been kidding herself when she thought that having sex with him would be the same as it had been so long ago. Perhaps there might be a kernel of her old lover buried deep inside him, but the outside was foreign—and just a touch scary.

Jill vowed to keep their relationship on a friendly basis. She'd thought she wanted to talk to him about the kiss they'd shared at the hospital. Now she'd rather they both just forgot it. It simply couldn't happen again.

Soon, she'd ease her guilt and find a way to tell him about Andy. After that, together they could discover new ways to deal with each other as their son's parents. Period.

Today, she *would* keep a steady head. She *would* learn to sail.

That's all there was to that.

A half hour later, Jill's head swam with all the instructions about tacking, which buoy to keep on which side of the boat, and who has the right of way when you encounter a powerboat. Her thoughts seemed scattered, not at all like her usual self. She couldn't concentrate anymore. Perhaps it was the sun, beating down on her head and frying her brain.

Reid must have noticed her sudden quiet, because he lifted an eyebrow and scrutinized her. "You doing all right?"

She wasn't positive how she was doing.

"You're getting too much sun. Even though it's a cloudy day, you'll burn." He quickly moved inside the cabin.

It was cloudy today? She pulled off her sunglasses to glance up at the sky overhead and found only tiny patches of blue, mingling with the multicolors of gray and the threatening black.

Reid returned, took the tiller from her hands and handed her a bottle of SPF-30 suntan lotion.

He sat down opposite her again. "What's happened to you? When we were kids, you always had a tan. Your skin got so dark back then that it lasted all winter."

She shrugged. "There's not too much sun in a court-room or buried in a law book."

After managing to unscrew the cap, Jill fumbled with the bottle and dripped more lotion on the boat than she did on herself.

"Here let me," he offered. "The wind's died down a bit. Just hang on to the tiller, but don't worry too much about our heading." Reid grabbed the bottle and pushed the wooden bar her way.

He poured lotion into his palm. "Stick your foot up on my knee."

She propped her foot and waited... And waited. Static electricity charged the air, and her nerves went on edge.

Finally, she lifted her head to look at him. His hand was frozen about two inches above her shin and his gaze was locked on her thigh.

"Reid?"

"Wha...what?" He had to clear his throat to speak, making Jill wonder if he felt the same tension that she did.

"The suntan lotion?"

He grinned sheepishly, but the smile didn't put the calm back into his eyes, now ebony colored and flowing with molten fury. Moving with deliberate care, he eased his hand onto her calf and began rubbing the liquid into her skin with circular motions.

Without warning, the humid, steamy heat turned erotic. Jill flushed with the fever of need and shivered with the chills of desire. She demanded that her body behave and attempted to cram the sudden ache of arousal down into a hidden corner where it had resided ever since Reid kissed her.

She gave her body a shake and tried to remember all her good intentions. *Sailing.* She must learn to sail. *Andy.* She had to tell Reid about his son.

But, oh, how this man oozed raw sensuality. His coarse fingertips skimmed over her tender skin and the sensations they caused called to something primal and elemental within her. Her only thoughts were of having those fingertips on other parts of her body, the ones now tightening and sensitive beyond bearing.

Reid moved to the other leg and glanced up at her, his dark eyes burnished with raw desire. She gasped, sucking in air and shaking her head. This had to stop.

"Aren't you finished yet?" she whispered. "Don't you think I'm covered well enough?"

"No," he answered with a rasping voice. "But I don't think I can stand much more."

The smack of the sails against an unexpected gust of wind caught both their attention. She jerked her leg to the deck with a thud. Reid stood to watch the horizon, turning his broad shoulder back to her.

"I suspect we'll be getting that rain you wanted," he warned, as he capped the suntan lotion and pitched it into the cabin.

Jill scrutinized the horizon and coughed to clear her throat. "Is that rain over there already?" She pointed to the far western edge of the lake.

Reid nodded, pulling down hard on the brim of his cap and placing his hands on his narrow hips. "Want to run toward the storm? It'll be good practice in tacking."

She silently acknowledged that both concentrating on her lessons and flying across the water with the wind in her hair might be just what was needed to clear her head. Somehow she had to calm her shattered nerves.

He drew the lines attached to the two sails through a cleat to tighten them and handed her the ends. "There you go. Let's see what you've learned."

Bracing her legs, she held the lines in one hand and grabbed the tiller with the other. Following the wind turned out to be a real challenge, as well as a lot of fun.

The sleek sailboat skated long the tops of the waves when the billowing sails tightened with the rush of air currents. At times, the wind proved to be stronger than she was. Jill had to wrap the lines from the sails around her wrist so that she could hang on to the tiller with both hands.

She found herself exhilarated and laughing—shrieking into the gusts as she moved the boom from port to starboard while Reid scrambled to stay out of the way. She hadn't had this much fun in years.

In a bit, Reid waved at her to slow the boat down. Disappointed the ride had to end, she let the lines loose and the sail luffed in the changing breeze.

"We're a little too close to the shoreline," Reid called to her.

He'd moved up onto the bow once again and gazed down into the darkening waters. "I sort of remember where the channels are, but it's been a long time. I'm sure you'd rather not run aground, skipper."

Jill didn't think that sounded like much fun. Being stuck out here would be embarrassing. She swiveled in her seat to look for other boats that might be available to help if necessary, and was surprised to find that the few others she'd noticed earlier had all disappeared.

The shore didn't look particularly inviting either. They were drifting past a part of the lake where limestone bluffs rose twenty feet straight up from the shallow waters.

"Drop the jib sheet altogether, and turn hard to port...go left. We're about to miss the channel," Reid yelled.

She jerked on the rudder and let go of both lines, feeling the sloop's forward motion slow.

"Not *that* way. The other left." Reid turned to her, at the same time reaching to brace himself against the mast.

"The *other* left? What..." Jill started to question his directions when the sailboat came to an abrupt halt with a sickening thump.

Deathly silence filled the air. The only noise was the soft lapping of still waters against the sides of the now inert boat. In the shallows and lying dead in the water, the smells of rotting fish and freshwater debris filled the air and closed in on Jill's senses.

"You forgot that 'left' means 'turn the rudder to the right.'" Reid broke the quiet with a grin aimed at her.

"Are we stuck here?" she asked.

"We'll see." Reid slowly moved back to the bow, unfurling the smaller, jib sail as he went.

When he finished, he came back to the stern where Jill sat watching him work.

"What can I do to help?"

He chuckled low in his chest. "Nothing at the moment. I'll let you know what to do when I need it."

Reid tore the cap from his head and threw it toward the cabin hatch. Reaching down to pull his T-shirt's hem from the waistband of his shorts, he yanked the garment up and over his head. Then with one swift movement, he vaulted over the transom and splashed into the water next to the boat.

Jill jumped to her feet, shocked at the sudden move

and the fleeting sight she'd caught of the man's muscular chest, covered by a patch of thick dark hair. He'd actually gone into the water still wearing his khaki shorts.

The splash of cold water against his overheated skin caused Reid to utter a single, sharp and descriptive oath. But as he stood, waist deep in the crystal clear shallows, he realized the drastic change in temperature wasn't having the desired affect on his ferocious and growing need.

"What are you going to do?" Jill leaned over the side of the boat to check on him.

Ah. What he wanted to do and what he was going to do were miles apart. This was a fairly public place and she hadn't made it clear that she wanted him to make a move yet.

As Jill bent over the side to peer into the water, his eyes were drawn to her blouse's open V neck. The top button had come undone and Reid's resolve slipped a notch as well.

Two rounded mounds of pink-toned flesh swelled delicately above the lace edge of her blouse. A sharp, sudden pull ran swiftly to his hard arousal. He opened and closed his fists and breathed deeply.

With an immense effort at internal control, he waded around the sloop to find the deepest spot. "We're going to rock this boat back into the channel."

She moved to port, shadowing his movement within the boat. When she was no more than a few inches from his new position, she stopped, holding his gaze with those stunning eyes, the very same color as the lake on a bright day. He found he couldn't take the painful intimacy of the moment and glanced toward the shoreline to get his bearings.

Breaking their connection made him feel like a downright coward so he quickly looked back, only to catch her appraising him with an approving, wry smile on her lips. Seems Jill was having some of the same distracting thoughts he was having. Good.

Reid stood still and did a little more appraising himself. The breeze tousled her curls and a stray strand of hair blew across her lips. His hand gripped the boat's edge as he fought the urgent demand to reach up, gently brush the unruly curls from her mouth and replace the silky stray strands with his lips.

He groaned with the effort of not letting his body move as it demanded and decided the immense pleasure of just looking at her would temporarily have to do. Wondering if he could tap the staggering volcano of burning hot sexual energy and adrenaline building inside him, he shoved hard on the side of the sloop and watched Jill's eyes grow wide as the boat rocked against its natural anchor.

After a couple more violent rocking movements, and with Jill's help on the tiller, the sloop slid back into the channel. Reid clamored back over the side and landed with an undignified thump on the deck.

''Wow! That was terrific. But…'' she looked both impressed and wary.

He stood, steadied his breathing and moved aft. ''But what?''

''Do all sailboats get stuck in the shallows like that?''

Smiling at her, he decided to tease. ''Only if their skippers are inexperienced…or are distracted by a beautiful woman.''

She blushed the most exquisite shade of rose, competing with the sun for color in her cheeks.

''But Travis's yacht would be too big for me to push off. What should I do then?''

"Yacht?" Reid was suddenly very interested. "Just how big is Trav's boat?"

"Well, I think I heard him say that it's nearly fifty feet long. I know it's the biggest schooner on all of Lake Austin. That's why the governor expects to be aboard on Saturday."

"Jill, you can't skipper a fifty-foot yacht. At least, not with only a couple hours of lessons on a twenty-foot sloop. Besides, you'll need a crew to man the sails on her. And a schooner that size will have auxiliary engines. In fact, you won't even be under sail for the parade."

"Oh." She looked a little taken aback, but he could see the wheels turning under those soft, dark curls. "Then *you* be the skipper and I'll be the hostess. I'm sure Travis has a decent crew all lined up that we can use."

Reid considered the implications. That would be one way for him to do a little undercover work at the regatta and fund-raiser.

"Okay. I'll do it. But in that case, you really don't need anymore lessons, do you?"

She shook her head slowly, looking a little forlorn and disappointed.

"I'll bring us in," he murmured, hating to see that look in her eyes, but needing to leave her heady, sensual temptation and go back to work. "Maybe we'll get a chance to sail together another day."

He raised the sails, took control of the tiller and began slowly negotiating the shallows. He wanted them back on the main part of the lake and headed toward the shore before he stopped thinking altogether, gave in to his instincts and took her in his arms right here.

"Look," Jill shouted.

Reid's gaze followed her pointing finger, just in time to catch the line of opaque rain moving across the tops of the waves and coming like an onslaught of rotary blades directly towards them.

By the time he moved the tiller again, the driving rain hit their sloop and swung the aft section around violently. The sails were less than useful, and Reid had the fleeting sensation of impending disaster.

# Nine

Jill never would forget the way Reid's eyes turned deadly serious as he'd spotted the purple and black threat of an approaching storm front.

"Uh-oh." He left the tiller and dashed up to the mast, unfurling the mainsail as he went. "It's coming too fast for us to outrun. We'll have to sit it out." He'd hollered at her to be heard over the roar of the sheets of rain, pounding against the churning lake water and steamrolling in their direction.

"Wonderful!" She felt the excitement race up her spine at the same instant she noticed the first drops of rain hitting her arms. "I can't wait."

"This is serious." He threw her a frustrated look, finished tying up the folded sails and reached into a storage compartment, dragging out a heavy metal anchor.

At that moment, a flash of lightning split the sky. Two

seconds later, the rumble of thunder crashed frighteningly around them.

They were alone on the bay. No other boaters were stupid enough to stay out in such a terrifying storm. Together, on their small boat, they faced the elements of nature by themselves.

The rain began for real. Jill leaned her head back, closed her eyes and stuck out her tongue.

"Ahh," she moaned. The cold prickles of rain against her sensitive tongue were as thrilling as when she'd been a child.

Another crash of thunder and the heavens opened, spilling out the life-giving liquid and returning needed moisture to the earth.

"Let's hope the anchor holds." Reid grabbed her arm. "Come on. We're going below. It doesn't offer much protection from the lightning, but at least we won't drown in the rain."

He dragged her in the direction of the stairs heading down to the cabin. The boat lurched with a slight roll and the wind swung the stern back around hard, daring the anchor to give way.

She lost her footing and fell into him, realizing for the first time that he was still minus his T-shirt. He never slowed down but slid his strong arm around her waist, steadying her as they headed for the shelter of the tiny cabin.

Reid moved through the hatch first, jumped the three narrow stairs into the cabin below and turned to help her down. She'd just placed her foot on the top rung when the boat pitched once again, throwing her off-balance. Jill tumbled down the short staircase, closing her eyes to await the crunch of knees on the hull bottom when she landed.

Only the crunch never came. Instead, her hands hit a solid, warm wall of pure muscle. At the same time, sturdy arms molded around her, steadying and unnerving her.

Jill's eyes snapped open. Mere inches separated them. And that was suddenly too much space to suit her. She splayed her hands across the searing flesh of his chest and drove her fingers through the coarse, dark hair.

"Uh. It's too tight in here for us to stand, you'd better sit down, honey." He tried to back away, watching her carefully. "I'll find us some towels to dry off." Reid's voice was barely audible.

"No. I want you to be right here."

"Jill." He sighed her name and covered her hands with his. "I've wanted you for such a long time. Seems like forever. Don't say things like that unless you're sure about what you want."

Even with panic and excitement fighting inside her, she stepped closer, anxious to feel the warmth of him.

"Please don't ask me to be reasonable and sure, Reid. I don't want to think right now. I want you to make me stop thinking." On a moan, she breathed a prayer that he wouldn't ask for explanations or demand promises she simply couldn't make.

"Another few seconds and I can't guarantee I'll be able to stop anything," he murmured.

"I don't want you to."

He folded his arms around her and drew her into his embrace. He held her like a fragile doll, yet as he breathed into her hair, she felt his powerful male presence, giving her intensely feminine and decidedly sexual sensations deep inside.

The two of them could never again have a committed relationship. There was too much in their past—too much between them in the future. They'd been separated far too long, become different people, with different needs.

Jill knew all her reasons meant she should back away before he wanted something more from her than she could give. Whatever else he'd done or not done in his life, she knew he was honorable enough to let her go if that's what she demanded. But she wanted this moment. Needed it like she needed the rain.

Ferocious cracks of thunder noisily exploded through the sky. The wind thrashed against the boat, rocking it wildly. Jill sucked in a breath at the thrill of the wild, savage elements of nature. Reid crushed her closer to him, keeping her enclosed within the safety of his arms.

Wet bodies and dripping clothes melded together with a steamy kind of heat. The tingling feel of his hard thighs against her own softening body, drove her into a sensual haze. Her bones liquified. Her knees refused to hold her.

Reid's heart leaped into his throat. He backed her up a step and gently guided her down on the narrow bunk. She was unsteady on her feet, but he was afraid his wouldn't hold the two of them either.

He stood beside her, reached for her face and drew aside a soggy curl that had matted itself to her cheek. He tucked it behind her ear, but he couldn't force his hand away from the satin of her jawline. She leaned her face into his open palm and breathed a sigh.

His eyes devoured her, taking in every detail. His gaze came to rest on her eyes and searched them, needing answers, but not wanting to wait for them.

"Make love to me, Reid," she whispered between breaths.

That same old tingling sensation took over his body and he relaxed into it, easing down beside her. The first thing he'd dreamed of doing was tangling his fingers in her hair. He watched her eyes grow wider while his fingers stroked and sifted through the luxurious black curls.

Taking a steadying breath, he let the scents of rain, musky sweat, and the hint of herb perfume, still lingering in the air, wash over him. No, he couldn't wait for the right words from her, maybe it was still to soon for her to know how much she loved him. But he knew it. Knew it like he knew every crevice and secret, sensual spot on her body.

He'd dreamed of this for far too long. They didn't need words for such a momentous occasion. What he needed was a strength of body and spirit to show her what was in his heart. To take the time necessary to prove that he worshiped her.

The low, dull ache in Jill's belly intensified as Reid's brilliant eyes took on a typical male gleam of appreciation. That look became all the promise Jill needed.

She gave way to the driving impulse that had consumed her ever since the first riveting glimpse of golden brown skin now quivering under her fingers. She let her palms roam over his wet shoulders and down his chest, kneading the hard muscles and reveling in the slick sensuous flesh.

He closed his eyes and groaned—a deep rumbling from within his chest that competed with the thunder for her attention. The sound stirred her senses to new heights. She loved the feel of him, and let her hands move over every inch.

Her fingers unexpectedly encountered an indentation that felt like an old wound. He hadn't had any scars marring his body years ago, and she wondered what had happened to give him such a slash.

Within moments, she found several more old scars, jagged and angry. She started to ask him to explain, but remembered in the nick of time that there were some things she wasn't ready to confess to him. Deciding this was not the right time for *anyone's* questions, she leaned in and placed a light kiss against one of the ragged marks instead.

"You need to get out of these wet clothes," Reid said with a wink.

Never letting his eyes leave hers, he reached for the buttons on the front of her soaking blouse. His big hands fumbled with the tiny buttons as she felt both his trembling need and his frustration with the time consuming task.

"Let me," she said shakily.

She began undoing the blouse from the bottom up, savoring his frustration and the anticipation of the sensual promise of skin on skin. Her breasts began to swell, tightening into aching prominence.

And still, his dark eyes held hers with a steady-as-a-rock gaze. His lean, hard-boned features intensified the devastatingly masculine awareness with which he scrutinized her.

The back of his knuckle grazed her breast as he continued to tug on the buttons. She licked her lips in response, making him groan again. He gave up his struggle, dropped one hand to her waist and used the other to tenderly brush away a trickle of rainwater from her cheek with his thumb's raspy pad.

"Please...take it off," he said hoarsely.

She ripped at the rest of the buttons and shrugged out of the shirt in record time. A cool whisper of humid air wafted across her bare, wet shoulders and she shuddered.

He reached for her again, pressing his lips to the column of her throat. At first, he placed gentle, light kisses on her neck and shoulders, occasionally licking at the rivulets of water cascading down from her soaking hair. But soon his mouth began to claim, devouring her in hungry, arousing kisses.

His mouth commanded. Her gooseflesh rippled in response.

Placing a searing, soulful kiss on her lips, his hands moved to span her rib cage. The sight of her lace-covered breast, full and crested with pouty, rose peaks jutting toward him, made his breath quicken. He should have known his Jill would wear lace under lace.

Everything about her and about their relationship was complicated. But Reid was determined to show her how simple and basic the passion between them could be.

He wanted her to lose control. That way she'd be free of her misgivings and become vulnerable to his spirit. His love surely must've been imprinted upon her soul long ago. He knew her love had resided in every cell of his being from the time he'd been nineteen years old.

He bent his head to lathe her nipple through skimpy material. She sucked in a breath and reached for him with a frenetic movement.

He pulled back and gazed at his darling love. "Easy, honey. All things happen in their own time. I've carried your memory around for ten years. Give me a chance to experience you for real."

Slowly, barely touching her, he skimmed his fingers over the edge of the lace bra, lightly tracing the curve of her breasts. Watching her eyes light with desire, he fingered her nipples through the flimsy, see-through covering, softly pulling and rolling them between his thumb and forefinger.

When she fisted her hands at her sides and closed her eyes, he slid the thin bra straps down her shoulders, unclasped the back fastener and removed the last obstacle to the sinful, satiny sensations he'd been craving. Her eyes opened when the humid air bathed her naked skin in cool sensitivity. She jerked her arms across her chest to cover herself, but he gently tugged them back down.

''No, luv. Please just let me look at you. It's been so long. You're so beautiful.''

Helpless, Jill could hardly bear to sit still while his gaze swept over her. But she managed to remain motionless as he held her arms to her side and perused every inch. The erotic caress of his loving look made the blood rush under her skin, tantalizing and sensitizing every inch.

Finally, when she thought she might not be able to stand the assault of his gaze for one more minute, he reached out to reverently touch her breasts. Sliding his palms under the curves, he held their full weight gently and with exquisite care. She felt delicate and adored.

When he began again to explore her skin with lazy, patient hands, her head fell back on a moan. Then his tongue replaced his hands and she jerked as the sensations moved directly to her gut, setting up a throb between her legs.

He exhaled hard and swore under his breath while he licked and nipped her swollen tips. She was so responsive, so sexy. The smoldering desire had darkened her eyes to a midnight blue and began to drug him with need. He cautioned himself to give her more time for relearning their love—their passion. His own needs be damned.

Her hips bucked as he sucked a heated nipple deep into his mouth. Impatience flared and he grabbed the waistband of her shorts and panties, ripping them down her legs, tossing them behind him. It wasn't so much the outside covering he wanted to remove, but his inner being demanded that he strip her to the very essence of her soul.

Finally, she was there before him as he remembered her. And he did recognize every inch of his lover. Patience, he warned himself. There was a time for everything.

This was the time to explore the edge of ecstasy. To bring her to an age-old place of pleasure and massage away all her doubts. Slowly.

He stroked the tender skin on her upper thigh, watching as her whole being rippled with relaxed joy the same way it always had. Placing one hot palm flat on her stomach, he could feel the shudders moving along the deep recesses of her body. Reid was transformed into a conductor, playing a symphony along the plains of his darling's passion.

"Please," she begged. "I need…"

"Yes, my love," he whispered, blowing on the silken flesh below him. "I know what you need. I need, too. But I'm only just getting a good start on telling you how much."

With infinite patience and experienced care, he touched her in places she'd forgotten she possessed. His hands sculpted her muscles, lingered on tender spots. With gentle urging, he brought her to the edge, only to soothe and smooth until she floated back down again.

She was greedy to share this slow burn with him, to take pleasure from watching him writhe under her hands and lips. But Reid wouldn't allow it. Every time she reached for him or began to place a fiery kiss across his skin, he lightly pushed her hands away.

He licked the dripping water from her body, beginning with her toes and moving up her shins to the responsive flesh of her inner thighs. Soon, along with the pulse beat of desire thrumming at her very core, she began to feel cared for, watched over—and loved. Her body responded to his ministrations exactly the way it always did in her dreams. And her heart urged her to remember their soulful unions of the past.

Reid had to tap the immense reserve of control he'd built up over his life alone to refrain from becoming too greedy. Whenever he was tempted to rush, to release his own building fire, he tasted her downy skin once more. Spun honey and fine cognac.

Filling himself with her unique flavors was enough for the moment.

Anxious to sample all of her tastes, he encircled her thighs with his huge hands and spread them wide enough so he could slide between. He slipped a hand under her hips, kneading the silkily tight flesh and lifting them toward him. Blowing lightly over her feminine mound, he smiled as Jill jolted in response.

No longer able to contain himself, he tenderly opened her intimate folds the same way he would peel back the petals on a delicate rose. Finally, he took pleasure in drawing his tongue across the engorged and sensitive bud he found waiting for him. Jill squealed and shook with heated delight.

Letting himself have the treat he'd craved for what seemed like forever, his tongue stroked and his lips sucked the velvet at Jill's core.

She screamed into the howling wind and pleaded with him for the release of the fire consuming her bit by bit. A lightning bolt illuminated their little nest through the tiny portholes, electrifying the air and contrasting its violent onslaught with Reid's slow ministrations.

With a murmuring sigh, he shoved his shorts down and onto the floor then slid up her body, leveraging himself on his elbows until her flushed face was directly below his. "Jill," he reverently whispered her name.

Her legs came around his waist and the look in her half-opened eyes was glazed, tantalizing and erotic. But he wasn't done teasing, preparing her for the love he wanted her to know throughout her entire being.

He allowed his throbbing arousal to nudge her slick opening. Then slowly, carefully, he entered her. By now he was desperate to feel the tight glove of her body surround him. Still, he vowed not to rush.

Half an inch inside—and he withdrew. Jill's breath caught and he watched her try to focus on his face.

Bending his head, he brushed a light kiss over her lips to still her protests. Then with more control than he thought he possessed, he gradually entered her cavern once again. Only to withdraw—just as unhurriedly as before.

Using the shallow-deep thrusting method of the ancient Taoist erotic masters, he continued to bring them both to the very edge of oblivion time and time again. She tried to buck her hips against him, begging him with her movements, but he reached below her once more and, with one hand, held her rounded bottom tightly in his grip.

At last, Reid could stand it no more. Sliding fully into her waiting warmth, he stilled—rejoicing within the blessed tightness and nearly crying out at the pleasure of being joined with the woman of his dreams.

Jill's whole body was afire with little pinpoints of sparks. Never. Never had she thought that being with a man could be so consuming. Her dreams of Reid had recalled a passion and a fire of desire, but this...

This was unspeakable pleasure, an unknowable drive to fulfill a wild and savage command.

He linked his fingers with hers and they began to move

together in a building tempo that suited their intense rapture. Before, Jill imagined that she might spontaneously combust with the flames he'd kindled. Now, her vision blurred with passion and she held on to the cosmic fireworks, riding the explosion to the top of crest. Finally, she detonated in a shower of burning light, calling his name over and over as he swept them both cascading past the pinnacle.

Jill's limp, sated body lay entwined with Reid's and she placed a soft kiss against his throat. The howling storm outside began to subside while the two of them tried to steady their own rapid breathing.

Vaguely, from the back of her conscious mind somewhere, she remembered the jarring thunderbolts of lightning illuminating the cabin as they'd made love. The wind and waves had rocked their boat wildly, but neither of them paid much attention.

The scattered, crashing blasts of nature matched what was happening inside them. The thrill of being at the mercy of the elements couldn't compete with the spine-tingling intoxication of his hands and mouth on her skin.

He stirred, eased back from her and leaned up on an elbow. The loss of his warmth distressed her.

"Don't go." She slid her arms around his neck and pulled him down to her.

Reid chuckled. "I won't go very far away, sweetheart. We're not finished here. But right this minute, I think I'd better check on the boat before we make love again."

"Again?" She swallowed a gasp. "You're kidding."

Leaning his forehead against hers, he whispered lightly over her still heated skin. "No, ma'am. One afternoon certainly won't be enough of you to fill me up...a lifetime might not do it either. But quitting now would only leave us both wanting.''

He pushed up, picked up his shorts and pulled them over his hips. ''And we've both spent far too many years in that state already, thank you.''

Gazing down on the dazed eyes and swollen lips of the woman he loved, Reid wasn't sure he could manage to make a cursory inspection of the boat before his body clamored for him to rejoin their two souls. But for safety's sake, he figured he had to try.

He reached past an interior bulkhead and pulled a towel from a secured compartment. With tender care, he covered her head and rubbed lightly over her hair, drying the excess moisture and warming himself with the friction against his palms.

''Dry off a little, honey. I'll be right back.'' He handed her the towel and ducked under the cabin's hatch for his quick trip to the deck.

Reid scanned the horizon through the softly falling rain. Not another sign of humanity was visible. He worked his way through the rigging, checking on the sails and lines. All seemed to be in order aboard their floating love bed.

He returned to the stern and tugged against the anchor rope, hoping it would continue to hold them for a while longer. It seemed secure, so he swung back to the cabin, not willing to be separated from Jill's warmth for one more second.

''Is everything all right?'' She stood, half in and half out of the hatch, looking up at him.

He nodded and reached for her, but before he could grab her up in his embrace, she scooted out onto the deck. And that's when he noticed she hadn't put on any of her clothes.

Staring down at her naked body, he felt his own stir beneath his shorts. She waltzed around the deck, holding her arms out to encompass the gentle wind and rain. Throwing her head back to blink up at the drizzle, she drank in the delicious mist.

Reid smiled. What a little imp she was. His body hardened as he watched her prancing around, her dark curly hair hanging loosely down her back and a decidedly feminine swing in her gait.

In a few moments, she lay flat down on the passenger bench and closed her eyes against the heavier droplets of water. "Hmm," she purred.

He went still for a long second, then sat down on the opposite bench almost afraid to breath. "Just had to feel the prickle of raindrops all over you, didn't you?"

She nodded, but when she opened her eyes, the heavy-lidded passion he found there tripped him up and ran past all good reason.

As he dropped his shorts on the deck, he watched the water run down her breasts and move into the same crevices he wanted to revisit. She opened her eyes to peruse his body, moaned and raised her arms, beckoning to him.

When he didn't move to her fast enough, she touched him, stroking and rubbing with unbearably erotic stimulation.

"Wonderful," she murmured, just before she arched her back like a cat and lazily spread her legs apart.

That was the all the invitation Reid needed. Gathering her in his embrace, he let the undulating movement of the boat under her hips drive them both to a slow, second burn. The snap of static electricity, left behind by the lightning, hummed down the mast and contributed to the sizzle he felt running through his veins.

At the zenith of their lovemaking, as she gripped him

deep inside and cried his name, he realized Jill was as essential to him as life itself. Too soon, she lay whimpering while he cradled her in his arms, both of them totally spent with shattering release.

Reid pressed a kiss to her temple and wondered why he'd suddenly been struck by a flickering sensation of guilt. He loved her with everything he had to give, and even though she had yet to admit it, he knew she loved him with the same glittering intensity.

So the guilt was a surprise. It certainly wasn't about anything they'd done together.

All right, so maybe he'd neglected to use protection, but frankly, if she became pregnant from their coupling this afternoon, he'd be glad. Grateful, even. He'd give the whole world to have a little brother or sister for Andy, and to watch his darling Jill grow round with a child—their child.

After giving it some more thought, Reid knew the problem. He'd been lying to her. Even if it was for his job at Operation Rock-A-Bye, he simply couldn't let a lie continue to come between them.

Before he told her that he loved her and that their futures were destined to be entwined together forever, the truth of who he was and why he'd really come home would have to be revealed.

A hollow sense of foreboding rose in his chest and he had to close his eyes against the sensation. Fighting the cold, dark intuition, he tightened his arms around the only person that had ever really mattered in his life, shutting out the entire world and along with it, a haunting portend of loss.

# Ten

**S**unlight glinted off the rippling waters of Lake Austin and bounced against stark-white, billowing sails as Jill watched Reid and Andy help the crew of *Bennett's Pride* secure the yacht to its moorings. Her heart had twisted like the red and black flags atop the many masts when she'd spied father and son working together.

It had been two days since the most spectacular sailing lesson of all time and the guilt was slowly, and without mercy, killing her. She still loved Reid with her whole being. No question about it. Though, she realized making love to him before he knew about his son had been a very foolish thing to do.

The guilt that had held her back before now threatened to destroy her. Never in her life had she let so much time go by before doing what needed to be done.

She turned back to the lake, gazing out at the spectacular sight of a hundred sails moving like multicolored ballerinas over the choppy waters on this perfect late June day. The air fairly reeked of politics and the lingering scents of power and money.

The parade was done—the regatta underway. The governor and Bill would be delivered to the reviewing stands and in a few minutes, she and the two most important men in her life would be able to slip away to the rodeo.

All things should be in perfect order. But of course, they were far from it.

Why hadn't she had the courage to tell Reid about his son in all these years? The night after that magnificent sailing lesson, she'd vowed to tell him the truth the very next day. Unfortunately, Reid had left town first thing in the morning, saying he'd had a problem at work to see to, but that he'd be back by parade time.

So she'd spent the last two days mulling over the best way—and the best time—to tell him about Andy. During those long hours without him, she'd also figured out some of her motivations for not seeking him out during the last ten years to tell him the truth.

Mostly, it was her stupid pride. And, if she really wanted to be truthful with herself, a touch of revenge came into the equation as well. She'd been dumb enough to want Reid to pay for the pain he'd caused her by withholding the joy of watching their beautiful child become a young man.

She sighed aloud, but the breeze scattered the sound in much the same way that her thoughts were jumbled and disjointed. Pain from his youthful rejection still stung, despite her overriding love for the man he'd become. And despite her well-deserved guilt.

The feelings were all tied up with her father's rejection and dismissal when he'd sent her away to Paris. If it hadn't been for her cousin Travis's kindness after her return, she probably would've sworn off of men forever. Maybe she still should.

"Hey, Mom." Andy, skipped over to stand beside her. "Reid says we're all set to change for the rodeo."

Jill placed a palm against her child's cheek, remembering that there would always be at least one man in her life—one young man to whom she also owed a lot of explanations.

But Reid had to be first. She only hoped that both of them would eventually forgive her.


"What's Travis doing here, Jill?" Reid kept one hand firmly holding onto Andy's shoulder while he directed his gaze to the box seats right above them.

Andy twisted and jiggled up and down, trying to break free long enough to run to the railing of the calf-roping ring.

Jill took hold of her son's other shoulder to get his attention. "Stand still. Reid will take you over to meet his friend in just a second."

She looked up at Reid's dark eyes, nearly invisible under the brim of the black Stetson he'd pulled low on his forehead. "I don't know." She threw a glance over her shoulder to Travis and a couple of other men seated in the best seats in the stands. "I mentioned to him that the three of us would be coming after the sail parade today. Maybe he thought it sounded like fun."

"If he'd wanted fun, why didn't he skipper his own yacht this afternoon?" Reid shook his head absently. "Trav never cared much for the rodeo back in school. Why the interest now?"

She shrugged her shoulders. "He said he had to work with one of his legislative committees this afternoon and that's why he couldn't make the parade. And as to why the interest in rodeo now... I have no idea. But I can ask him while you take Andy to meet your old friend.''

"Legislative committee?'' Reid's eyebrows went up. "I thought the lawmakers were on summer hiatus.''

"They are,'' she admitted. "But he's chairman of a permanent committee with oversight responsibility for the state's Department of Child Protective and Regulatory Services. Seems like Travis spends more time with them than on anything else he does for the legislature.''

Reid shot one more thoughtful look toward Travis, then smiled at Andy while he addressed them both. "We won't be gone long. The rodeo can't come to a complete halt just because two cowpokes want to talk to one of its calf-roping stars.''

Andy twisted out of his mother's grip. "Yeah, Mom. We need to go *now*.''

Jill laughed at her son's excitement, even though she knew her carefree times with both of them were quickly coming to an end. After they took Andy back to the ranch this evening, she had plans to tell Reid the truth. Andy's turn would come tomorrow.

"Don't worry about Andy and don't go very far, sweetheart. Stay near Travis.'' Reid bent to place a blazing kiss across her lips. "When we get back, I believe it'll be about time for Andy to call it a night.''

He winked at her and the gleam in his eyes made them turn that shiny, ebony color they got when he was aroused. "You and I have some things to talk about later.''

Yes, my love, she thought, as she swallowed back a sob of panic and regret. We most certainly do.

Reid had always loved the sights and sounds of the rodeo. The roar of the crowds in the stands. The whirring colors of the buckskins and roans as they kicked up dust, obscuring the fans' view. The giant screen, broadcasting their antics to every corner of the arena.

He breathed in the sweet fragrances of sawdust, leather and sweat, both man's and animal's, while he guided Andy past a retaining wall and into the area behind the chutes. Normally, the strains of country music playing louder than necessary and the crackling energy of the waiting competitors' nervous tension combined to rush adrenaline through every part of his body.

Tonight he had too much on his mind for any such luxury. As he and Andy searched through the mingling cowboys, all waiting their turns to compete, he tried to sort through the various thoughts and emotions all clamoring for attention in his brain.

He should have told Jill who he was long before they ever made love. Failing that, he should have told her immediately afterward.

He frowned at the thought. Too damn much misplaced sense of duty, he derided himself. This overriding need to do everything by the book, to make sure the path was right and the way was clear, might be the death of him yet.

Spending the last two days informing his FBI superiors that he would be breaking cover long enough to tell Jill the truth about himself, then rushing Intelligence to do a speedy minimum security check on her, kept him from doing what his heart knew was the right thing. Simply telling her that he needed her and wanted her to marry him.

Tonight, no such compulsions would stop him. After ten long years, the time was finally right again.

"It kinda stinks back here, don't it?" Andy dragged Reid by the hand as they passed the roughstock pens.

"No worse than the foaling barns when they're all closed up for winter," Reid answered with a smile.

But he knew what the boy meant. A few seconds ago, they'd walked by the concession stands with their mouth-watering smells of Italian sausage, fried onions and cotton candy, and the contrast with the animal smells could knock you down.

Fortunately, at that moment, his old buddy Clayton McCloud came into sight.

"There he is. Hurry up!" Andy jumped with excitement at meeting one of his idols.

Reid greeted his old friend and introduced Andy. Clay sure looked a lot older than the last time he'd seen him.

The thought reminded Reid of the many wasted years without Jill. So much unnecessary heartache. All about to finally be put behind him.

"You on track in the circuit standings again this year?" Reid asked his champion friend.

"I expect I have enough points for the Buckle, if that's what you mean." Clayton pulled a pair of leather gloves from the back pocket of his slightly too-tight jeans. "But this'll be my last year for competition. I'm retiring."

Andy's eyes were round with wonder and admiration. Reid suppressed a chuckle and breathed a silent prayer that someday the boy would gaze up at him with that very same wide-eyed admiration.

For most of his life, Reid had been secretly hesitant to become a father, determined not to rush into making the same mistakes as his own father. But this child made the whole idea seem easy. And definitely worth all the effort.

"You're giving up the spotlight?" Reid poked the cowboy in the ribs and threw him a broad grin.

Clayton chuckled and drew on a glove. "My body won't hold out much longer, old buddy. Besides, it's time

I gave back some to the sport that's done so much for me."

"Really? What're your plans?"

Reid watched Andy hanging on every word.

"Well, you ever heard of the Little Britches Rodeo?" Clayton asked.

"Sure," Reid answered. "They've been doing good work with kids for years."

It was Clayton's turn to beam. "Right. They've asked me to come on board. Work with the youngest children, help develop new programs."

Reid slapped his old friend's back. "Wonderful! I'm impressed. You'll be doing a great public service."

A buzzer sounded over the distant applause of the crowd.

"That's my cue. I'm up." Clayton smacked the glove he'd been holding against his chaps, turning quickly to Andy. "Sorry, we didn't get much time to visit, kid. Maybe I'll see you at one of the Little Britches training camps."

Andy bobbed his head up and down with gusto. "Yes, sir. I sure hope so."

On the long walk back to the stands and Jill, Andy was subdued. Probably dreaming of his future and of winning a silver buckle of his own some day.

Reid was grateful for the few minutes of relative quiet. A couple of things pertaining to Operation Rock-A-Bye had been niggling at the back of his mind, and he wanted a chance to sort through them before he totally gave up on thinking altogether when he and Jill had their long-overdue talk.

Being on board that hugely expensive yacht today had made him curious about how his old friend Travis had become so filthy rich in the last few years. Then seeing

Trav tonight with a couple of men who looked more like they belonged on America's Most Wanted list rather than at a rodeo, only served to stimulate his curiosity.

And what was it Jill said about her cousin spending much of his time on the Department of Child Protective and Regulatory Services committee? Just over a year ago, a couple of his Operation Rock-A-Bye agents captured a woman on the Texas-Mexico border who ran one cog in the international baby-selling racket.

That woman had been using her position as an area director for the department to bring non-U.S. babies across and give them legitimacy by placing them temporarily in nearby foster homes. When apprehended, the woman tried to strike a deal with federal prosecutors, but she hadn't known enough about her superiors in the organization to lighten her sentence.

She'd always claimed the big boss was someone high up in the Texas department that protected children. But Reid could never find any evidence of wrongdoing by any one of those hardworking bureaucrats, men and women who selflessly gave of their time to make sure neglected and abused children in the state were nurtured and adopted out to deserving parents.

So… Wealthy, powerful Travis Bennett was chairman of the department's legislative oversight committee? Now wasn't that interesting.

Reid needed to make a couple of phone calls. Which he promised himself he would do, just as soon as he gathered Jill and Andy up and ushered them away from these crowds and out into his truck.

As they rounded the path past the last taco stand, Andy tugged on his hand. "Reid, I've been thinking."

Reid slowed and waited for whatever the boy had to say.

"You know just about everything and everybody that's worth knowing in this whole world," Andy said.

"Well, maybe not everything," Reid amended, grinning at the boy's serious demeanor.

Andy ignored him and continued with what seemed to be a little speech. "I think you'd make the very best dad a kid could ever have. Do you think that might happen someday?"

"What…might happen?"

Andy puffed up his chest and squared his shoulders. "That you'd be my dad."

Reid's heart flipped and he ached to hug this special, little boy. He remembered just in time that at Andy's tender age, hugs were only allowed by moms—not between men.

Needing to clear his throat to say what was in his heart, Reid eventually answered one of the most important questions he'd ever been asked. "I can't think of anything I'd be more proud to do in my life than be your father, Andy." He stuck out his hand to shake. "Let me work on your mom a little bit. I'll see if it can't be arranged."

From her seat in the stands, Jill watched Reid and Andy make their way back to where they'd left her. God, she loved them both so much. Seeing the light in their eyes go dark as she told them the truth, would be the hardest thing she'd ever have to do in her life.

Being deserted before her wedding, finishing law school part time, and raising a child alone were a snap compared to watching the pain in her loved ones faces when they realized she'd been lying to them for all these years.

She forced her wobbly legs to propel her down the

stands' creaky stairs, then waited in the wide aisle with as close to a smile on her face as she could manage. In less time that she cared to think about, all her smiles might be gone for good.

She deserved everything she got—and more. What kind of a horrible person would keep the truth from the men she loved? If they would let her, she'd work every day for the rest of her life to make it up to them.

Andy tugged on Reid's hand and danced his way over to her. "Mom! It was great. Mr. McCloud even talked to me."

"That's wonderful, son. Did you thank Reid for introducing you?"

Andy nodded and grabbed her hand with his free one. "Wait'll I tell you what Mr. McCloud said."

Jill knew, if she let him ramble, they'd be standing there for the next hour while Andy told her every detail. "You can tell me all about it later. Right now, I think we probably need to be going. It's almost your bedtime."

She glanced up at Reid, who stood patiently holding on to the hand of her gyrating son. But he wasn't looking at either of them. His attention seemed riveted to the stands behind her.

"Reid?"

He jerked his chin around to ask his own question. "Where's Travis, Jill?"

"He left as soon as I reached my seat near him. His cell phone and pager went nuts…apparently there was some kind of computer foul-up back at the office and he had to go see about it."

"Computer glitch…on a Saturday night?"

She shrugged a shoulder. "I guess so. Travis has an extra shift of people who work odd hours on special computer projects for him."

"Law projects?" Reid probed. "Or legislative projects?"

"I really don't know." She shook her head and tried hard not to look as foolish as she felt. "Computers aren't exactly my thing. I manage to use them for law research, but anything harder than that sort of loses me. Travis handles the computer department."

Reid looked up in the stands again, absently rubbing his jaw with his free hand. "Did the men that were with him leave as well?"

"Yes." She shuddered remembering the creepy appearance of the two characters Travis never managed to introduce before they all left. Day-old beards, greasy hair and Armani suits all seemed way out of place at a rodeo.

"Do you know who they were? Friends of Trav's, maybe?" Reid's voice got stronger, his words slightly clipped and harsh. "Were they clients, Jill?"

"I really don't know." She shook her head and raised her shoulder blades. "I'm pretty sure they weren't friends."

"Mother!" Andy impatiently pulled his hand from hers and swung that arm in a circle. "I have to tell you about the kids' rodeo."

"Don't interrupt, dear. Later, you can…"

"But, Mom, Mr. McCloud said there's special camps for kids, and junior rodeos…and that maybe he'd see me there…and everything!"

Jill glanced up at Reid. "What…?"

"Clayton is retiring after the last event on this year's circuit." Reid's eyes softened and he chuckled lightly. "He was telling Andy and me about joining up with the Little Britches Rodeo. And…"

Andy jumped up and down, pulling his hand from

Reid's and clapping wildly. "He said he'd see me there. Didn't he, Reid? I can go, can't I Mom?"

Reid squatted down, looking the bouncing boy right in the eyes and lowering his voice to calm him down. "I'm sure that when you turn eight, your mom will consider letting you take one of their training camps."

"Eight?" Andy drew himself up in huff. "I'm no baby. I'll be ten on my next birthday in January and grown-up."

"Well, then," Reid began with a smirk. "Give your mom and me a chance to find out more about..."

Every noise and every movement in the whole arena seemed to still as Reid stopped speaking and stared at the young boy's face in front of him. Even Andy apparently sensed the need for quiet. He glanced up at his mother with apprehension. Jill forgot to breath while she watched Reid making the connections and counting back the years.

Silently he glanced down at his clasped hands, elbows resting on his bent knees. She could see that his knuckles were whitening as he gripped his fingers together.

At last, he looked up at her, the pain and confusion visible on his whole body. "Jill? Why didn't you tell me?"

Uncomfortable and confused himself, Andy moved out of earshot over to the arena's fence and soon became engrossed in the girls' barrel riding. Jill let him go.

"I'm so sorry, Reid." She managed to say on a half sob. "I swear I didn't realize I was pregnant before you disappeared. And I should have told you sometime during the last ten years, but...I..." Her voice was raw with emotion, and the words died with her despair.

"Then he *is* mine." Reid bolted upright, fisting his hands, his words a statement more than a question.

But those hard words and betrayed glare widened the hole that was burning through her heart. "Of course," she choked through the haze of pain. "There's never been anyone else."

Jill's brain was a jumble of emotions. Guilt at having kept the two of them apart for all these years was the overriding one. Everything was all her fault. She'd wanted so badly to find a way to save her relationship with both father and son. And now everything was ruined. Both might hate her forever.

Was there some way for her to make amends—even at this point? She had to try. The two of them needed each other, and she needed them. Desperately.

"Reid." The words would be difficult. "Forgive me for not telling you all these years. I was angry. My pride got the better of me."

He stood in silence, rod straight with his hands still fisted at his side. He wasn't going to make this any easier. He'd probably never forgive her.

Deep in her heart, she knew that she'd probably never be able to trust him with her heart again either. But she would trust him with her life—and her son's. That would have to be enough.

"I want you to be his father. I want the two of you to get to know each other now. Don't punish him for my wrongs."

Finally, he managed to speak through gritted teeth. "Just what would you suggest at this late date?"

"Why don't you take him to your mother's ranch for a few days? Get to know each other better. The only thing I ask is that you wait to tell him the truth until I can be there."

"Neither one of us needs your lies anymore, Jill. I'll tell him when I think the time is right."

Without another word to her, he strode over to Andy. "How would you like to spend a few days with me on my mother's ranch...son?" Gentling his words, he turned his back on Jill.

Wary hope lit Andy's eyes and he glanced around Reid's body to the woman holding her breath. "Can I, Mom?"

Building tears blurred the sight of her sweet son while the guilt of not telling him the truth nearly overwhelmed Jill. "Yes, Andy. I think that would be fun for you. But I need another minute to talk to Reid right now."

Keeping his broad back to her, Reid bent on one knee to talk to his son. "Andy, why don't you go get us a couple of corn dogs?" He pulled a few bills from his shirt pocket and handed them over. "Give me a chance to talk to your mom."

"Go ahead, sweetheart," she said, with as much calm in her voice as she could manage. "But just don't forget what I've told you about strangers. Be careful."

"Yes, ma'am." Andy took off, unmindful of the currents of pain and anguish circling the two grown-ups.

The man she'd loved for most of her life stood stock-still in the middle of the wide aisle and stared at her with a mixture of disbelief, hurt and disgust on his face.

"You stole ten years of my son's life from me," he roared at last. "And we made love, but you never once..."

His whole body shook with frustration, and he pulled off the Stetson to wipe his shirtsleeve across his eyes. "I thought you cared. How could you keep my son from me? From his grandmother?" Reid's eyes glinted hard and cold. "And to lie to your own son, for God's sake?"

"Listen to me, please," she cried in earnest. "I fought with everyone in my family, trying to find you. When you left, I was devastated, my pride destroyed. But I swear to God, Reid, I did everything I could to find you…to tell you…until Dad and Mom forced me to leave for Paris.''

He narrowed his eyes at her. ''There never was another man in Paris?''

She shook her head vehemently. ''Never. That was a story Mother told around town to save my reputation. You've got to understand. When I came home, everyone believed it…. And you were living somewhere else, married to another woman.''

Grabbing his arm, her knees buckled. She let her gaze plead with him for some kernel of compassion.

Reid shook her off like he was shooing away some annoying bug.

''I'm taking my son home to get to know his other grandmother. I'll tell him the truth his mother never thought important.'' At her gasp, he spat out one more hurtful statement. ''I think maybe you'd better get yourself a good child-custody lawyer. I certainly intend to do so.''

''Hold on, Reid. Remember I'm an attorney…and his mother. You wouldn't stand a chance in court.''

He turned his back on her and searched for Andy in the crowd. ''We'll see, Jill.''

''Don't do this, please.'' She reached to touch his arm, but once again he jerked away. ''I don't want to fight you. No one would win. I want what's best for Andy.''

Without another word, Reid walked toward his returning son. She couldn't possibly bear to face him in a court.

Jill dropped her hands to her sides and slumped. She deserved every bit of this. But, oh dear Lord, the pain was excruciating.

# Eleven

"I understand that your pride is hurt, son." Reid's mother slammed a cookie sheet onto the worn-out butcher block counter in her kitchen and reached for a spatula. "And, of course, you have every reason to be indignant."

Taking a deep breath, Reid figured he was in for a lecture. In the two days since dropping Jill off at her mother's ranch and driving away with his son, he'd given himself enough lectures to last anyone a lifetime. He'd sort of hoped that his mother would take his side and go easy on him. But sympathy was apparently not on her agenda this afternoon.

Holding one edge of the sheet with her favorite "antique" kitchen rag and shoving the burnt-edged, wooden spatula around with the other, June Sorrels spoke her piece. "I mean, you being so *honest* and all." A little biting sarcasm served with chocolate chip cookies was exactly his mother's style. "To me…it seems like a man who's never told a lie should have the right to expect everyone else to treat him with the same respect."

"Very funny, Mother. You know that my job is the reason I have to make up stories. I'm undercover in order to bring criminals to justice. It's not the same thing at all." Reid reached over to snag a chocolate chip cookie before she could shovel it onto the waiting platter, only to burn his fingers in the process. "Ow."

"Hmm." She set the spatula down and drew him to the sink and placed his hand under the cold water faucet. "I'll bet my grandson knows the difference between a lie and the real truth. And I'm positive he has more intelligence than to get his fingers burned stealing cookies."

She shook her head, leaving his hand under the running water as she picked up the scraper once again. "Now, just *how* did I go so wrong with you?"

Her eyes crinkled at the corners, twinkling with obvious delight, even though a frown turned down the edges of her mouth.

Standing here in the old kitchen where he'd been raised, smelling the delicious aroma of baking cookies and hot apple crisp, Reid fervently wished that his life had turned out the way he'd always hoped. He'd give anything not to have become this jaded, fatigued captor of bad guys—one who'd not only learned to lie easily, but who'd also been forced to make his mother learn to lie for him.

She'd never complained about telling friends and neighbors made-up stories about what he was doing for a living and why he hadn't come home in over ten years. But it had always hurt to ask her to lie for him. Hurt deep inside where he'd buried all the distasteful things from his past life.

A mere two days ago, he'd made the decision to begin living his life by the truth again. And he'd been planning on starting with Jill.

Now, he couldn't even face the prospect of telling Andy that he was his father. Some truths seemed harder to tell than others.

"Cookies!" Andy burst through the back door, his boots still caked with cow manure. Streaks of sweat and hard-earned dirt colored his face and neck.

Reid's heart nearly popped right out of his chest with love for this child who was all boy, yet sweet and considerate enough to capture anyone's heart.

Except—when there were chocolate chip cookies involved.

Taking after his father, Andy reached for the still too-hot platter only to be swatted away with an old kitchen rag. "Ouch, Grammy." He looked emotionally stung by the woman who'd asked him to call her Grammy even before he knew the reason why. "Can't I have a cookie, please?"

Her face dimpled into a broad smile. "You *may* have lots of cookies…"

He started to reach again and she grabbed his hands in both of hers. "*Just* as soon as you wash these hands and take off the hat and those filthy boots."

Andy frowned for a second then grinned up at her. "*How* many cookies?"

She tsked at him and pursed her lips to keep from laughing out loud. "Lots. And I have a special treat, too."

His eyes widened.

"Some good boy, who comes back into this kitchen

with boots off and hands scrubbed clean, will get to lick the mixing bowl if I haven't already washed it by then. You have any idea who that'll be?''

"Me!" He took off, clopping across the linoleum at a gallop. "I'll be back in a minute."

Reid watched his mother smiling at the disappearing back of his extraordinary son, and found himself wishing they'd had so much more time together. *All* of them.

He'd finally gotten hold of his pride enough to realize Jill had only done what anybody would have done under the same circumstances. She'd been young and in trouble, and the person she'd thought she could count on to be there for her had disappeared.

It nearly undid him to remember her wounded look, standing there in the middle of a crowded arena aisle pleading with him to see the past through her eyes. Her pale face and the haunted cast in those crystal blues seared him with an ache that he'd been wallowing in ever since.

Part of his pain had come from guilt. From allowing his pride to stop him from going to her in Paris when he'd been released from the hospital all those years ago.

Reid didn't doubt for one minute that *she'd* tried to find him at first. The real question in his mind now was why her father had been so adamant that she stop looking. Had he known what his daughter would've found?

"You going to tell Andy today that you're his father?"

His mother's rather chastising tone of voice broke into his thoughts. "I'm not sure I have the words, Mom."

"Oh, for goodness' sake." She went back to the oven, opened the door and checked another batch of cookies. "The words will come from your heart. You think too much."

Before he could argue his point and explain how he

couldn't bear to see the hurt in his child's eyes when he found out his mother had been lying to him for his whole life, Andy appeared in the doorway. Hair combed, feet clad in socks only, and hands held out palms up for inspection, he smiled shyly at his irascible grandmother.

"Was that fast enough? Do I get to lick the bowl?"

"Sure you do. You win. You're the fastest and cleanest kid in all of Texas." She went to him, wrapped an arm around his shoulders and guided him to the kitchen table. "You start on this bowl while I get you a glass of milk."

She set the mixing bowl in front of him and turned around to Reid. "Would you like some cookies and milk now, too?"

He chuckled at his mother's tendency to use food to soothe away any problems. But he sat down opposite his son and dug into the platter of cookies with gusto, just the same.

"Yes, ma'am. I sure would," he mumbled past a cookie.

She busied herself getting glasses and milk, all the while talking over her shoulder to her grandson. Both Reid and his son would've had trouble answering any questions with their mouths stuffed with cookies and dough, but she never asked them any. She simply babbled on about baking for people who appreciated her efforts.

When Andy was done with the bowl, he moved on to the enormous mixing spoon. His grandmother poured him another glass of milk.

"You ever thought much about your real, true father, boy?" she asked as she put away the milk carton.

Reid nearly choked on a chocolate chip. Andy just nodded and took a sip of milk.

"Yeah, I figured you had," she said, and threw Reid

a keep-your-mouth shut look. "What do you think he'd be like?"

"I know what he'd be like. He'd be 'xactly like Reid is."

"Oh? How do you know that?"

"Mom told me," Andy mumbled through cookie dough. "She said he was big and strong and knew about everything."

"Did she say anything else?" Reid couldn't help but ask one little question of his own, even if his mother did smack him along side the head with the rag.

Andy thought about it for a second. "She said he wanted to help people and that he'd never lie to anybody on purpose…and that she'd loved him very much."

Reid's mother rested a hand on her grandson's shoulder and spoke gently. "You know, Andy, sometimes things don't work out the way we want them. Sometimes people accidentally hurt themselves and others when they don't really mean to."

Andy nodded and reached for another cookie. "Oh sure. Like when I fell in the bull's pen. I didn't mean to get hurt or to scare Mom, but it just happened."

"Right. Like that." She sat down next to him and waited until he looked at her face. "What would you say if I told you that Reid *was* your really, true father, and that he didn't mean to stay away from you so long, but things accidentally turned out that way?"

Andy shot a glance at Reid, hope coming alive in his eyes. Then he turned back to his grandmother, looking decidedly thoughtful and too grown-up for his own good.

"Mom knows you're telling me this, right?"

Reid held his breath. His own mother had started this, and he prayed she had a good way to finish.

She smiled at Andy and put a hand on his arm. "Yes,

son, she does. But she hasn't known how to explain it to you. Parts of the story are complicated and you need to be a little more grown-up to understand.''

A very long and suspenseful couple of seconds later, Andy jumped up and ran to Reid. ''You're really my dad?''

Reid chanced a hug and whispered in his son's ear. ''Yes, son. I'm your father and I love you very much. I'm sorry I haven't been a part of your life in the past. But now that I've found you, I promise we'll never be apart for long again.''

Andy drew back and studied his father's face. Reid wondered what truths or lies he saw there.

''Should I call you 'Dad'?''

''Certainly, you may.'' Reid's heart turned real flips. ''Or maybe you'd prefer 'Papa'...or 'Daddy?' Call me whatever feels best to you.''

The truths of a child's life came simple and unhampered by old guilt or remembered slights.

''Way cool!'' Andy moved back to his grandmother's side. ''Can I have a cookie now, Grammy?''

Jill lowered her cheek to the cool, shiny surface of her mahogany desk. Coming in to work today had obviously been a mistake. But being at the ranch with her mother's I-told-you so's and her own conscience nagging at her had been more than unbearable.

Talking to Andy on the phone hadn't helped much either. He'd babbled on about Reid being his ''really-truly'' dad, and she never could hear any blame in his voice. She needed to talk to him in person, but she didn't want to spoil his time with his father. Mrs. Sorrels had invited her to the ranch several times. Jill couldn't bear the sight of Reid's disdain, so she'd declined.

She closed her eyes and fought the images she'd imagined of Andy's face as he learned of his mother's mistakes. How long would it take before he stopped hating her deep down inside, she wondered?

The phone on her desk buzzed loudly next to her head. She dragged herself upright and forced her hand to pick up the receiver.

"Jill?" Her caller was Bill. "You sound terrible."

Shaking her head, she wondered what else life could do to aggravate her today?

"Yes, Bill, it's me. Thanks for reminding me of how bad I feel."

"I hope you're not sick," he mumbled politely, but then never gave her a chance to deny or confirm it.

"I heard a terrible rumor this morning, Jill. And I want you to tell me that it's not true."

"You know better than to believe everything you hear," she cautioned him.

"Well, this came from a particularly reliable source." Barely taking a breath, Bill started in with his interrogation. "I want to know if Reid Sorrels is your son's father. I've heard the stories about you two coming close to a marriage some years ago. But I thought the deal fell through at the last moment."

Jill cringed. There was only one "reliable source" who could have told Bill. Her loving cousin Travis.

"Is it true that you weren't married to Andy's father? And if so, was the story about the husband in Paris also a fabrication?"

"Yes, Bill," she sighed. "All of that is true."

"I see." He followed that pronouncement with a couple beats of dead silence. "Look. I don't want to appear to be a rat deserting a sinking ship, but you must know that a political campaign can ill afford to have any scandal lurking around the corner.''

"Yes, Bill," she managed. "I understand."

"Good. Because then you can understand why I'm forced to fire you as my campaign manager. I've already contacted a party professional to take over in your place. I'm sorry, Jill, but I have to watch my backside. You know that."

"Yes, Bill," she said through clenched teeth. "I know that your backside is the most important thing in the world to you. And I sincerely hope you two will have a long and fruitful life together."

She slammed down the phone and hung her head in her hands. *Men.*

The first one to betray her was Reid when he left with no word. Next came her father when he turned a cold heart to her pleas for help in finding her lost fiancé. Then Reid showed up, only to break her heart all over again. Now, foolish Bill Baldwin was cutting off an easy path to the governor's mansion with her as his chairman just because of his injured pride.

And then there was Travis. Her cousin had been acting so strangely lately. What was with him, anyway? Normally easygoing and competent, lately Trav seemed scattered and distant.

This morning she'd tried to talk to him about her heartbreak and fear over what Reid would say to Andy. But Travis had cut her off, claiming he was swamped with troubles in his computer department. For the life of her, Jill couldn't understand why he didn't just hire someone to solve his problems. Or what the heck was so important that they couldn't get along without the computers for a few days?

And then for Trav to betray her by telling Bill about

Reid... Well, all men were jerks. She vowed to be done with them forever.

All of them except Andy, of course. She just had to pray that he wouldn't decide to be done with *her* forever.

Like a miracle of faith, at that exact moment, Andy burst into her office with his usual youthful exuberance.

"Hiya, Mom. Guess what?"

Her throat threatened to close with the emotion of seeing her only son standing within inches and smiling as if he hadn't a care in the world. She could do nothing but shake her head in amazement.

"Grammy Sorrels says we can all come live on her ranch if we want. She bakes the very best cookies in the world, you know. Dad says she can cook all kinds of good stuff...and she knows how to rope steers, too. Not just calves, but big giants...and she puts brands on them and everything!"

Andy finally had to take a breath and Jill quickly reached for him, tugging him close. "I take it you had a good time, son," she said, smiling into his hair.

Without releasing her grip on Andy, she glanced up and found Reid leaning against the door frame and grinning with the silliest expression on his face. With no hat, his silver-tipped hair hung casually on his forehead. Dressed in jeans and a long-sleeved western shirt, he looked as young as the first day she'd met him—over half a lifetime ago.

She gently placed her hands on her son's shoulders and set him back far enough so that she could see his face.

"Isn't it great about Reid being my dad?" Andy wiggled out of her grasp. "Now we can all live together forever. You were right when you said God will answer your prayers if you're good and ask real nice."

She touched her son's warm hand to satisfy herself that

he was truly there—and seemingly not angry at her at all. But welling tears kept her silent and biting on her lip once more. There wasn't much chance of them all living together. Not with Reid hating her forever.

Reid stepped closer. "Sorry to just barge into your office like this, but…" He placed a hand on Andy's bare head and rolled his eyes with phony exasperation.

He gazed down on his own soul in the form of the beautiful woman who'd stolen his spirit so many years ago. He wasn't sure exactly what to say to her to let her know she was his whole life. How to tell her what was in his heart? He only knew that lies would have to stop coming between them. There was too much at stake now.

"Uh. Can you take the rest of the afternoon off, by any chance?" he asked over Andy's bobbing head.

She stared up at him with a mixture of stunned confusion, lingering hurt and perhaps a little bit of love. That last feeling was the one Reid wanted to explore—and maybe to build a life upon.

"Ye…yes," she stuttered. "I guess I can. Why?"

"I think you and I should have a long conversation. There's something important that you need to know about me."

Her eyebrows narrowed, but she kept her gaze focused.

"But right now, can you close the office down for the day and drive Andy back to your mom's ranch? I have a small chore to do here first, then you and I can ride out to that little creek where we used to talk. Remember?"

"Of course, I remember." The look in her eyes softened but was still confused and wary. "But why can't you drive back with us?"

Without answering her directly, he slipped into his professional shell and got ready to face his nemesis. "Is Travis in his office?"

"I think he's back in his computer room," she said warily. "But I haven't seen him since this morning. Why?"

"This has nothing to do with you, Jill. Take Andy home," he urged. "I'll join you in a little while."

# Twelve

**R**eid found Travis alone in a back room, shredding papers and packing up boxes of computer diskettes and CDs.

"You won't get very far, Trav," he muttered as he stepped into the room. "We've got men surrounding the place, and everyone else has been evacuated from the building. Why don't you take your chances making a deal with the federal prosecutor? Maybe you'll get lucky?"

"You?" Travis plopped down in a nearby secretary's chair and stared up at Reid. "I should have known. Ever since you came back to town, things have gone to hell. And then Saturday when we noticed our security had definitely been breached, I figured the Feds would show up soon. That's why we destroyed all the hard drives this morning."

Travis waved his arm at a nearby easy chair, indicating Reid should help himself to a seat. "Any deal is likely not in my future, buddy. My…uh…'backers' from up north wouldn't let me live long enough to collect my end.'' He rubbed a hand roughly across his forehead. ''What agency are you with, Sorrels?''

''FBI. Though it doesn't really matter.'' Reid wondered if Bennett was armed and decided to remain standing for this little chat. The man looked haggard and nearing exhaustion.

''So, how'd you all of a sudden get so smart?'' Trav asked wearily. ''Or have you been trying to trap me into something for the last ten years and only just now got a clue?''

If he'd been the true professional he'd always imagined himself to be, Reid would have frisked his old friend, placed him under arrest and read him his rights. Instead, at the mention of old times, he felt compelled to probe Travis for some answers as to what happened on that fateful wedding eve so long ago.

''I guess I'm still not smart *enough*. What part did you play in what happened to me back then?''

Travis scrutinized him with a raised eyebrow, a frown and, at last, a heavy sigh. ''I suppose it doesn't matter anymore whether you know the truth or not. It's all over.'' He slumped farther down in his chair and crossed his arms over his chest. ''I knew you'd end up causing me trouble…ever since I first learned that those idiot goons I hired hadn't managed to actually kill you ten years ago.''

''*You* hired?''

Travis shook his head with an absent motion. ''Jeez. I guess I'll have to spell it out for you. I set you up, old buddy. You were *such* a goody-goody, and I had *such* a lucrative deal about to take shape with that character from Philadelphia.'' Trav smiled, shaking his head again.

"Well, I couldn't let you ruin things, now could I? Besides, your days were already numbered. There was no way in hell I would've let you become a partner in Bennett and Bennett. You weren't born to be one of us. You didn't deserve it."

Reid was flabbergasted. He'd reconciled himself to the fact that his old friend was now a crime boss, deeply involved in international baby-selling and murder, without scruples or remorse. But it never occurred to him that Travis had been this cunning and devoid of principles ever since they'd been kids.

"You hated me enough to kill me?" he asked somberly.

Travis waved the question off. "Hate has nothing to do with it. I certainly didn't hate Uncle Andrew, but I had no trouble at all ordering him killed when he got in my way. It's all a question of money, pal."

"Jill's father was murdered?" The revelations kept coming fast and furious and Reid had trouble keeping up with the evil spewing from the man he'd once considered a friend.

The look in Travis's eyes turned absolutely fiendish, and Reid felt his own hate and anger boiling up from some dark place within him that he hadn't known existed.

"One can order anything done...with enough money." Travis snapped his fingers. "Easy. Besides, the old jerk managed to piece together what was really going on with me and the firm."

Travis's smile became malevolent. "Dear Uncle Andrew belatedly realized I'd lied to him. For months I'd been trying to talk him into making what he'd thought would be a legitimate deal with that syndicate guy from Philly. But then that idiot knocked you out in front of Uncle Andrew instead of waiting until you'd left the house. So I had to tell Andrew that you two had been in cahoots and had lied to us both.

"A few weeks after that, my uncle figured out the truth." Travis's eyes glazed over with the memories. "With his daughter safely sent away, Andrew spent a couple of months checking the company's records. He was just about to turn me over to the authorities and begin searching for you.

"He had to go."

A red haze of fury rioted through Reid's veins. The man before him was the devil personified. He needed to be dead.

Fisting his hands, Reid shoved them in his pockets to keep from putting them around Bennett's neck and squeezing until the life ebbed away, taking along with it all the man's heinous acts against mankind—and saving the government a lot of trouble and expense.

Instead, Reid backed up a step, clenched his jaw, and slowly withdrew the weapon he carried in his waistband holster. He'd always sworn to defend and uphold justice. He would not take revenge.

Despite this almost incredible coincidence of Travis being the man Operation Rock-A-Bye had hunted for so long, Reid was relived that two mysteries had been answered with one capture. Travis was not the same man as the one he'd thought he'd known as a boy.

He narrowed his eyes, trying to judge if Travis would reach for a weapon, but the pitiful blob of humanity before him was obviously defeated. Reid was almost grateful to Travis for telling him the truth of what happened long ago. But not enough to offer him any significant advantage.

"You know it's all over, Trav. On your feet. I need to

read you your rights. Then you can call an attorney before we head off to find you a cell.''

The long shadows of approaching nightfall streamed across the wide Texas hillside, bathing Reid and his horse in dappled sunlight as he rode silently next to Jill, sitting atop her old favorite, roan mare. She breathed in the scent of cedars, hay and Fourth-of-July wildflowers.

Curiosity nagged at her from every side. Instead of showing up at her mother's ranch in ''a little while'' like he'd said he would, it'd been almost three hours later when Reid finally arrived and they'd saddled the horses. He'd looked like death warmed over, tired, haggard and beat down further than she'd ever seen him.

What had happened to him after she'd left was only one of the many questions she needed to ask. But he'd soberly asked her to wait until they were alone before he answered anything. Jill suspected he needed time to get his head together and figure out what he wanted to say. She'd remained quiet, but her mind raced ahead in full orchestration.

Had he gone to Travis seeking legal advice on how best to take their son from her? Did he want to share parenting responsibilities, or did he hate her enough to try stopping her from ever having any say-so in Andy's upbringing?

Her mind raced. She didn't want a court fight, *please God.* There had to be a way of working this out so that Andy wasn't hurt any more than he'd been already.

Stunned when Andy acted so casual after learning the truth, she figured you could trust kids to cut to the real meaning behind all the fuss. He didn't care one whit about the past. All her child wanted was a bright future that included both a mother and father—now that he actually had one of each.

Just when she thought she might explode with curiosity, their old meeting place next to the stream came into view. The willows by the side of its bank brought back memories of steamy kisses and passionate make-out sessions under its boughs. Light breezes rippled the tops of the tall, summer grasses in fields beside the stream, reminding her of their long walks and soul-revealing talks.

As they dismounted, she remembered that long ago they'd fallen in love at this place.

Turning to watch Reid's tall, broad figure while he tied the horses and pulled a couple of blankets from the saddlebags, Jill realized she loved him more than ever. As a girl, she'd been self-centered and controlling. She hadn't really been prepared for the kind of love she'd found in Reid.

Now, even with the fear that he might try to take her son, she knew that his was the only love that would ever matter to her in life. There could never be anyone else who touched her soul like he did.

But this time—she was strong enough and prepared enough to go on without him. Just as long as he didn't take try to take Andy with him when he left. She'd be forced to fight him, and that might destroy her relationship with her son.

He handed her a thermos of coffee and spread the blankets. She made herself comfortable as he poured each of them a cup of the hot liquid he'd begged from her mother's cook.

Longing for his deep-set, ebony eyes and practically drooling over the way his full lips moved over the edge of the coffee cup made Jill squirm in her jeans. This would not be the same as the old times they'd had in this place. Her dearest love was about to give her some very bad news, she could just feel it coming.

She straightened her spine and promised herself she wouldn't break down. If he was going to ask for her son, the least she could do would be to face it with a little pride.

"There's so much to tell you, Jill. I barely know where to begin." He glanced over to the stream and looked like he was about to say something they'd both regret forever.

She steeled herself a little more. "Did you see Travis?" she whispered and bit down on her lip.

"Yes, and telling you about that will be difficult, but first... I have something else I must get off my chest."

He watched her eyes grow round and her tongue peek out from the corner of her mouth as she tried to concentrate on his words. The little speech he'd practiced would be the absolutely hardest thing he'd ever had to do. Things like hiding in a dismal swamp for thirty-six hours while waiting for a suspect to cut and run or having to shoot a man you'd befriended in an undercover sting... None of that compared to the pain he was about to cause the woman who'd become his every reason to live.

"Jill, I've been lying for so long...and to so many people...that I'm not sure I can..." The confusion began to overtake the wariness in her eyes, and he forced himself to get on with it. "Look. I don't work as a bureaucrat for the Treasury Department like I told you. I'm really a special agent in charge for the FBI...head of one of their major undercover operations."

"The...FBI? You mean you're in federal law enforcement?" she stuttered.

"Yes, sweetheart. You want to see my ID?"

She shook her head. "I believe you, Reid. You never used to be a liar."

That small hurt couldn't possibly compete with the pain of telling her the whole truth. "I did stay with the law like I always said I wanted, Jill. Just not in the way we'd planned."

"But how...why?"

He found himself gazing down into the depths of the black coffee in his hand. If he had to look at her through this, he'd either break down and cry or end up smothering her in his arms before he finished. He had to tell her about her family. The rest could wait. But revealing family secrets could easily put a wedge between them forever.

"It's a long story. Just hang on long enough to hear me out. For the last six years, I've headed up an FBI undercover operation that was created to hunt down a very clever gang of kidnappers. Men who've been stealing babies from both sides of the Texas-Mexico border and selling them for top dollar to desperate and wealthy Americans unable to have their own children."

He took a hard breath and hurried to finish so he could take her in his arms—if she'd let him. "Following a promising lead, I came back to Austin in the guise of a bureaucrat on vacation, headed for his law school reunion. We figured the main boss of this syndicate had to be in the state legislature, and that maybe I could find him through my old friends."

Her confused and anxious look nearly stopped him cold. Somehow he wasn't telling this right. Unfortunately, he had no choice but to barge ahead the only way he knew how.

"I came back intending to use Travis...and *you*...if need be, to get our man." He rubbed at his aching jaw.

"I didn't have any idea what surprises were waiting for me here."

"You mean about Andy?" Jill's voice suddenly felt raspy, cracked and raw.

He blinked a couple of times, then softened his gaze. "Well, that. The identity of the man we'd been seeking...and a couple of other things, too."

Jill could barely sit still. She couldn't be angry with him for lying to her. She hadn't been the most truthful person on earth herself. At least his lies had been for the job.

The questions and confusion about why he chose now to tell his story were burning her from the inside out. How did Andy figure into this?

"So you found your suspect?" she ventured.

He nodded, and she wondered if that meant he'd been trying to tell her he was now free to leave—taking their son with him.

Reid glanced down at the ground and when he looked up again, his eyes were full of pain. "Jill, I can hardly believe this myself, but our suspect was Travis."

She could feel her head shaking uncontrollably. "My cousin Travis? No way."

As Reid patiently explained about Travis's kidnapping scam, Jill began to see the truth of how her cousin could've been exactly what Reid claimed he was. She didn't like it. After all, Travis had been the one she could count on for all these years. But the more she thought about his odd behaviors the more she believed.

When she was totally convinced, she began to worry. "Am I in trouble too? I mean, because I was his partner?"

Reid smiled. "No. It's clear he kept you and his legitimate business and political dealings separated from his illegal pursuits.''

She breathed in a long, cleansing breath. But her real concerns had not been addressed. All the men in her life were deserters or just plain bad. All but one. And she just refused to lose Andy. Not now, when everyone else was gone.

She couldn't stand the suspense any longer. "Reid, are you planning on taking Andy away from me? It would be terrible for him if we go to court.'' She hesitated, needing to clear her throat and get ready to beg. "I swear, if you'll give me a break, I'll find a way for us to share custody. I'll move wherever you want to live so we can be partners in his upbringing. I'll do everything the way you want it. Just please don't fight to take away our son.''

"Take him?'' Reid's dark eyes searched hers with something akin to a confused glare.

She ventured one more plea. "Just talk to me about it first, please?''

He grinned and reached for her, but she shrunk back. "I have no intention of taking Andy away from you, sweetheart.''

The look of tenderness on his face made everything a thousand times more confusing and potentially more painful.

"I love you,'' he began. "I've never stopped loving you. I just had to clear away the guilt and the pride long enough to recognize it. I have no intention of going anywhere without you...and Andy. I want you and I to be married. To be together the way we were always meant to be.''

She looked so shocked, so stunned, that he needed to reach out to her. He wanted her to feel the love and the need in his heart through the warmth of his body. To give her the truth of his feelings with his kiss.

She remained outside his touch.

"Nnn...no," she stammered at last. "We...can't. I...can't.

"Can't?" Was it because he'd arrested Travis? Or had she decided she couldn't love him because he hadn't come looking for her all those years ago?

"We can be friends, Reid. Partners in caring for our son. But I won't marry you."

Fear and panic seized him. There was no way she could really mean this. Gruffly, he dragged her into his arms.

"But...you love me. I know it as sure as I'm breathing air. I can see it in your eyes when you look at me. I felt it within your body when we made love." He held her close, breathing in the sweet, seductive smell of shampoo and the old scent of herbs he'd craved for so long. "Why won't you marry the man who loves you—the father of your child?"

A very real desperation was beginning to creep into his voice and he fought to remain calm. "Don't let old problems stand between us forever, my darling. We have a son who needs us both...together."

She trembled within his embrace and shoved against his chest until he had to let her push back. Her eyes were bruised, tear-streaked and red from her constant brushing them with the back of her hands. He couldn't stand the icy determined look he spied behind the deep pain.

"I do love you, Reid. More than even I imagined possible. But..." She sniffed and set her chin. "It isn't guilt that will keep us apart... It's fear. I'm petrified that you will leave me again like you did before. I can't need any man the way I'm beginning to need you. The last time just about killed me.''

"Wait a minute. Let me finish explaining.'' Reid tried to keep the panic out of his voice. "I didn't leave you ten years ago. The night before our wedding Travis contrived to kill me. He muffed the job, but I was knocked unconscious and nearly every bone in my body was broken. I awoke weeks later two hundred miles away in a hospital bed with my jaw wired shut.''

He rushed to finish what he never thought he'd tell her. "It was Travis who was the liar. He…he even ordered your father's murder. He's an evil man, Jill.''

"My father's accident was planned? No…no! Please stop. I can't hear anymore.''

She looked stunned and like she might be about to go into shock, but he knew his Jill was strong enough to take it. He had to finish. Had to make her understand.

"Mom finally found me in the hospital and told me your father was killed…that you'd gone to Paris and married someone else.

"Jill…darling Jill… My pride was crushed along with my body. I thought you didn't care enough to come looking for me. Once or twice, I even imagined that you'd been in on whatever happened to me. I was hurt… devastated.''

"And the woman you married?'' Her voice was cracked, rough but still strong.

"My physical therapist. I turned to her for comfort. She was kind and I desperately needed to believe I was still lovable. It was totally unfair to her. I can't believe I managed to end that marriage in friendship, but thank God she was as wise as she was kind.''

Jill pushed the back of her hand against her mouth, trying to stifle a sob. This was the truth finally? It was

too much to take in all at once. Her father. Her cousin.
The guilt of not being there for Reid when he needed her
so badly. She began sinking into a pit of depression that
was far worse than the guilt of not telling him about
Andy.

He reached for her, but she moved away again. Too
soon. Too much. She could forgive him, but could she
ever really forgive herself?

"I can't," she moaned.

"Can't what?" Reid narrowed his eyes. "Can't forgive me? Can't trust me?"

"I'm sorry. I...just can't."

Battling back the urge to curl up in a ball and disappear
into her own despair, she ran toward her horse and back
to a life full of emptiness. She deserved far worse.

The next day, Jill had a visitor. Deputy Manny Sanchez stopped by on his way to give a deposition in
Travis's case.

"This is none of my business, ma'am, but I hate to
see my old friend hurting so badly," Manny said, as she
offered him a chair.

Oh God. She'd hurt Reid yet again. He would be so
much better off without her.

"Reid loves you and your son more than life. I can't
stand to see needless pain."

Manny scrutinized her from behind big chocolate-
colored eyelashes. "Yes. As I suspected. You're in about
as much pain as he is."

He sighed deeply. "You two belong together. Perhaps
you always have. And you have the boy to think about,
too."

"I'm no good for Reid. I've caused him too much
heartache. He'll never really forgive me," she sobbed.

"Love is a strange thing, ma'am. With two separate people it can be hurtful and miserable. But put those two together and it can make all the pain disappear."

Manny rose to leave, but added one more thing. "Maybe it all boils down to trust. Sometimes you have to decide if love is worth the risk."

A few hours later, Jill once again found herself under the willows facing the man she'd loved for more than half her life. Yes, she did love him. More with every passing minute. But could they learn to trust each other again? Could she risk letting herself need and be needed in that all absorbing way she knew it would be with him?

"Don't let Travis's betrayal spoil the rest of our lives, my love," Reid finally said as a single tear leaked from the corner of his eye. Jill's heart tore into little pieces.

"I know you've become strong and independent," he said over a cracking voice. "But you're my every reason for living…you've always been my soul…the better part of me."

He reached for her and the warmth she found waiting in his embrace had her collapsing against his strong chest, encircled in his comforting arms. Her soul recognized his, her body ached to become one with him once more.

They'd both been hurt by others' actions, and their own. It was past time for all the hurting to end. And way past time to give in to the physical desires she knew they both had suppressed for far too long.

"Just let me stay near you while you figure it out." He kissed her ear and whispered softly, "Let me prove my love…I beg you. Don't set me aside due to fear. I could never hurt you. It would be like ripping my own heart out."

She pulled back and, for the first time in his entire life, Reid felt a real pang of fear. "Jill, don't…"

''When?'' She tilted her head to gaze at him with those shimmering crystal-blue eyes, while the corners of her mouth curled slightly upward in a half smile.

''Excuse me? When...what?'' Cautious hope began to replace his fears.

She reached to grasp his shoulders then, dragging him back with her to the blanket under the trees. ''When are you going to shut up and begin proving it by making love to me? We've wasted ten years of desire-filled caresses and passionate kisses. I don't need to rethink those.''

He gazed down at her and saw the smirk in her eyes, so wickedly sexy he had to blink to believe it.

''All things happen in their own time, honey,'' he teased with a breathless sigh of relief.

Grabbing her up and placing a feverish kiss on her waiting lips, he told her in the best way he knew how, that he'd always be ready to make love to her...

Now and forever more.

# Epilogue

**A** soft, late summer breeze whispered through the star-studded Texas night, cooling Jill's heated skin and soothing her senses. Coming to such a blissful close, this had to have been the most magical of all wedding days.

She lay, steadying her breath against Reid's naked chest and wondering at how fast the years had fallen away—leaving only the same two souls who'd found everything they'd ever wanted in each other's love. He rolled them to their sides and twisted, spooning himself behind her. She could feel his heart pounding through her back, and the rhythm brought with it a life-affirming beating in her veins.

"Happy, my love?" he whispered against her hair.

"Mmm-hmm," she murmured, sated and smug in her love.

"You're sure you're okay about not having a huge shindig like you'd wanted the first time around?" His question wasn't terribly serious. She knew because they'd talked this over more than once.

"I'm positive. I really didn't want a big deal the first time either. That was Mom and Dad's idea." She turned her head to plant a kiss on his muscular bicep, and breathed in a heady scent of the aftermath of lovemaking.

She had everything she ever wanted—her dearest love and her precious son together forever.

In the last month, she'd gone with Reid to his Houston office to wrap up the paperwork for Operation Rock-A-Bye—and he'd come with her to the law offices of Bennett and Bennett to close the files and sell off the assets.

His bosses fought to keep him with the Bureau. Her clients had pleaded with her to keep her office open. But at no time did either of them consider anything but a completely new start to their lives together.

Jill giggled as he blew a heated breath over her sweat-soaked skin. Squirming, she ground her bottom into his groin. Immediately hard and desperately ready again, he just couldn't get enough of this raven-haired pixie who'd stolen his heart so many years ago. But he wanted time for a few more words before he followed his body's urging.

"Sweetheart. Are you really sure about all these changes in your life?" Ridiculous how much more he could want and love her with each passing second.

She flipped over and pressed herself into him, nuzzling under his chin and whispering against his shoulder. "With you running for Justice of the Court of Criminal Appeals next year...and both of us working to combine our mother's ranching operations, I'll have almost everything just the way I want."

"Jill," he breathed on a ragged groan.

She quivered in his arms, reaching out for the length

of him. He grew thicker in her hands and moaned with the delicious torture of her touch.

"There's one more big change coming to our lives, my love," she said with a sigh. "Uh...I hope you don't mind another little calf-roper begging you to teach them all your rodeo tricks. I only hope this time...it's a girl."

"Another child? Oh, my God, Jill. You are the most wonderful...the most beautiful..." The words stuck in his throat.

He swung himself over and entered her with one swift penetration, needing some way to show her what was in his heart. Taking them both to savage release with a frenzied coupling that demanded everything, he gave all there was to give and ended with the familiar exchange of souls.

In the aftermath, full of joy and the glow of truly being one with the woman he loved, Reid held his precious wife in his arms and realized that what he'd always said had been truer than he'd ever known.

*All things happen in their own time.*

\*    \*    \*    \*    \*

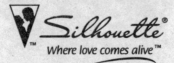

If you enjoyed what you just read,
then we've got an offer you can't resist!

# Take 2 bestselling love stories FREE!
# Plus get a FREE surprise gift!

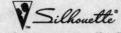

October 2002
## TAMING THE OUTLAW
### #1465 by Cindy Gerard

Don't miss bestselling author
Cindy Gerard's exciting story about
a sexy cowboy's reunion with his
old flame—and the daughter he
didn't know he had!

November 2002
## ALL IN THE GAME
### #1471 by Barbara Boswell

In the latest tale by beloved
Desire author Barbara Boswell,
a feisty beauty joins her twin as a
reality game show contestant in an
island paradise...and comes face-to-
face with her teenage crush!

December 2002
## A COWBOY & A GENTLEMAN
### #1477 by Ann Major

Sparks fly when two fiery Texans are
brought together by matchmaking
relatives, in this dynamic story by
the ever-popular Ann Major.

# MAN OF THE MONTH

Some men are made for lovin'—and you're sure to love
these three upcoming men of the month!

*Available at your favorite retail outlet.*

*Where love comes alive™*

Visit Silhouette at www.eHarlequin.com          SDMOM02Q4

# COMING NEXT MONTH

**#1471 All in the Game—Barbara Boswell**
She had come to an island paradise as a reality game show contestant. But
Shannen Cullen hadn't expected to come face-to-face with the man who had
broken her heart nine years ago. Sexy Tynan Howe was back, and wreaking
havoc on Shannen's emotions. She was falling in love with him all over again,
but could she trust him?

**#1472 Expecting…and in Danger—Eileen Wilks**
*Dynasties: The Connellys*
They had been lovers—for a night. Now, five months later, Charlotte Masters
was pregnant and on the run. When Rafe Connelly found her, he proposed a
marriage of convenience. Because she was wary of her handsome protector,
she refused, yet nothing could have prepared her for the healing—and
passion—that awaited her in his embrace….

**#1473 Delaney's Desert Sheikh—Brenda Jackson**
Sheikh Jamal Ari Yasir had come to his friend's cabin for some rest
and relaxation. But his plans were turned upside down when sassy
Delaney Westmoreland arrived. Though they agreed to stay out of each
other's way, they eventually gave in to their undeniable attraction. Yet
when his vacation ended, would Jamal do his duty and marry the woman his
family had chosen, or would he follow his heart?

**#1474 Taming the Prince—Elizabeth Bevarly**
*Crown and Glory*
Shane Cordello was more than just strong muscles and a handsome face—
he was also next in line for the throne of Penwyck. Then, as Shane and his
escort, Sara Wallington, were en route to Penwyck, their plane was hijacked.
And as the danger surrounding them escalated, so did their passion. But upon
their return, could Sara transform the royal prince into a willing husband?

**#1475 A Lawman in Her Stocking—Kathie DeNosky**
Vowing not to have her heart broken again, Brenna Montgomery moved to
Texas to start a new life—only to find her vow tested when her matchmaking
grandmother introduced her to gorgeous Dylan Chandler. The handsome
sheriff made her ache with desire, but could he also heal her battered heart?

**#1476 Do You Take This Enemy?—Sara Orwig**
*Stallion Pass*
When widowed rancher Gabriel Brant disregarded a generations-old family
feud and proposed a marriage of convenience to beautiful—and pregnant—
Ashley Ryder, he did so because it was an arrangement that would benefit
both of them. But his lovely bride stirred his senses, and he soon found
himself falling under her spell. Somehow Gabe had to show Ashley that he
could love, honor and cherish her—forever!

SDCNM1002